THE NEW HENNESSY BOOK OF IRISH FICTION

EVER SINCE INCURRING THE WRATH OF HIS FIRST EDITOR IN 1960 by making Hitchcock's *Psycho* his film of the year, Ciaran Carty has been a consistently independent and passionate commentator on film and literature, both as a reviewer and through his interviews with Irish and international artists in the *Sunday Independent* and later as Arts Editor of the *Sunday Tribune*. His first book, *Robert Ballagh*, a study of the artist, appeared in 1986 and *Confessions of a Sewer Rat*, a personal account of his fight against censorship and the subsequent development of the Irish film industry, was published in 1995 by New Island. He has been the editor of New Irish Writing since 1988.

BORN IN DUBLIN IN 1959, DERMOT BOLGER IS ONE OF IRELAND'S best-known writers whose ninth novel, *The Family on Paradise Pier*, was published in 2005. His tenth play, *From These Green Heights*, received the *Irish Times*/ESB Award for Best New Irish Play of 2004. A former factory hand, Playwright in Association with the Abbey Theatre and Writer Fellow in Trinity College, he received a Hennessy Award in 1988, was a judge of the Hennessy Awards in 1994 and in 2003 received the inaugural Hennessy Hall of Fame Irish Literature Award. He has been involved for many years in an advisory capacity with the New Irish Writing page under the editorship of Ciaran Carty.

Thirty-five years … Almost a lifetime when looking forward, but in many ways it seems like only the blink of an eye when looking back. So much has happened since David Marcus established New Irish Writing in the now sadly defunct *Irish Press*. We are pleased to have been involved with the Hennessy Literary Awards for all these years. These awards are unique in that they provide an opportunity for emerging writers and poets to be published in the *Sunday Tribune*.

Over the past thirty-five years many aspiring Irish writers have entered these awards, some of whom have established themselves as leaders in contemporary Irish literature, names like Joseph O'Connor, Hugo Hamilton, Colum McCann and Marina Carr amongst them. With Ciaran Carty firmly at the helm, this tradition of discovering and fostering new Irish talent has flourished at the *Sunday Tribune*. One of Ciaran's earliest initiatives saw the awards expand to include poetry, and this has helped to focus renewed attention on poetry in Ireland today. For this alone we should be grateful but Ciaran has added so much more over the years and is deserving of the many accolades bestowed upon him. We are also grateful to the Four Seasons for hosting our annual awards ceremony.

I am personally honoured to have been involved with the awards for many years and in that time I have had the pleasure of reading some fantastic work, as the contents of this anthology demonstrate. I invite you now to enjoy the work of some of the most talented writers in Ireland.

Maurice R. Hennessy
Director
Jas. Hennessy & Co.
Cognac

THE NEW HENNESSY BOOK OF IRISH FICTION

edited by DERMOT BOLGER *and* CIARAN CARTY

NEW ISLAND

THE NEW HENNESSY BOOK OF IRISH FICTION
First published 2005
by New Island
2 Brookside
Dundrum Road
Dublin 14
www.newisland.ie

This selection © Dermot Bolger and Ciaran Carty 2005
Introduction © Colum McCann
Individual stories © respective authors

The authors have asserted their moral rights.

ISBN 1 904301 33 9

British Library Cataloguing in Publication Data. A CIP catalogue record for this book is available from the British Library.

Typeset by New Island
Cover design by Fidelma Slattery @ New Island
Printed in the UK by CPD, Ebbw Vale, Wales

New Island received financial assistance from The Arts Council (An Chomhairle Ealaíon), Dublin, Ireland

10 9 8 7 6 5 4 3 2 1

New Island would like to gratefully acknowledge the financial support of Hennessy Cognac in the publication of this anthology

CONTENTS

EDITORS' NOTE

Ten years ago *The Hennessy Book of Irish Fiction* appeared from New Island, edited by Ciaran Carty and Dermot Bolger. It contained the first works by many writers such as Joseph O'Connor, Kate O'Riordan, Colum McCann, and others who made their debut in print in the monthly New Irish Writing page in the *Sunday Tribune* and who went on to either receive, or be short-listed for, The Hennessy Literary Awards.

New Irish Writing was originally founded and edited for many years by David Marcus in the *Irish Press*. The novelist and short story writer Anthony Glavin edited it during the last two years before the *Irish Press* closed down. In 1988 the challenge of maintaining this crucial outlet for each new generation of Irish writers was taken up by the *Sunday Tribune* and Ciaran Carty, who still edits the page today. The sole qualification for inclusion is that any writer submitting a story must not have already published a volume of fiction. Prose writers published on the page are automatically short-listed for the Hennessy Awards, which have been sponsored by Hennessy Cognac for the past thirty years and are exclusively devoted to honouring and supporting emerging Irish writers.

This second volume, *The New Hennessy Book of Irish Fiction*, contains our selection of some of the best work by writers who have had work first published in the New Irish Writing page in the *Sunday Tribune* over the past decade. Half these stories picked themselves. As editors we know that our selection of the remaining stories was subjective and that — due to reasons of space and occasional overlap in themes — it proved impossible to include a number of writers first published in New Irish Writing who would perhaps have equal claim to be represented here. Because the page is about publishing writers as they emerge, where possible we have kept the original biographical note from when the story was first published, followed by an updated note.

One of the first stories we each chose for this anthology, and one which had remained vividly in our minds since first reading it in manuscript form in 2000, was 'The Separation' by Paul Grimes. When seeking permission to reprint this story we were deeply saddened to hear of Paul's untimely death. Many writers published in New Irish Writing have rightly gone on to become internationally famous. Others have tragically been robbed of that chance. We wish to dedicate this book to the memory of Paul Grimes, Martin Healy (the short story writer from Sligo who received a Hennessy Award in 1994) and Noelle Viad (the Killybegs poet who received the Hennessy Award for poetry in that same year), all three of whom have been taken from us at far too early an age.

Our thanks to the Hennessy Family and the *Sunday Tribune* for their generous and continued support, to Michael Simpson at Edward Dillon Ltd, to the superb production team at New Island, and to all the emerging writers who, year in and year out, continue to make New Irish Writing such a vibrant barometer of the health of writing in Ireland today.

Dermot Bolger and Ciaran Carty
Dublin, October 2005

INTRODUCTION

Landing in the Deep End

Colum McCann

As a young man living in Texas, rottenly broke, I didn't have the money to go back to Ireland for the Hennessy Awards in 1990. The rooming house where I lived had a swimming pool. Sounds bourgeois, but believe me, it wasn't. It was my job to clean it and fix the broken filters. I had just shocked the water with chlorine and the pool was chemically clear when the phone call came from Dublin with news that I had won the award. I climbed the roof of the house and jumped, though not gracefully, landed in the deep end and swam for a moment underwater. I'd broken a surface and wanted to stay happily underneath for a while.

A few years later I walked from Dublin to Galway in order to try to meet Desmond Hogan, another Hennessy Award winner and one of my favourite writers. It wasn't so much poverty as pilgrimage that had me go on foot. I'd no idea if he'd be there or not. I'd heard rumours that he was living in a blue-roofed house by the sea. After eight or nine days I arrived in Clifden and found Hogan standing on a headland, getting ready to swim. He was surprised and laughed along with me – I showed him my backpack, my worn-down boots – and he asked me if I'd missed the bus.

Hogan had an everyday routine where he swam in the ocean. He swung his head and dived in. That was another day, too, that I jumped.

And perhaps that is the thing about the Hennessy Awards – that we swim in the wake of what we admire.

The best ones always sound, the first time, as if you've heard them many times before. You read a story in half an hour and you remember it a lifetime. There's nothing quite like the thrill of coming upon a new voice, whether it be already full or just beginning to sound out. We derive our voices from the voices of others. It is a sort of literary mitosis.

If I stack up the names of Hennessy winners off the top of my head – Neil Jordan, Patrick McCabe, Dermot Bolger, Deirdre Madden, Mary Morrissy, Joseph O'Connor, Marina Carr, Mary O'Malley, Anne Enright – it becomes a roll of what has proved to be lasting. There are few other awards I can think of where new talent is not only found, but manages afterwards to mature and thrive. It's not so much the money, God knows – though it did help me find the silence and time for a novel. And it's not the brief crackle of fame. No. It is much more the heritage that's involved, the sense that the writers are going forth on a journey and it just might be that they will return, stronger and changed, with even more to say.

It is the job of writers to confront the times they live in, to give no echo to the worn-out, to come up with new ways to stun. This collection is a great rattlebag of promise, but already some of the writers have stamped out a territory for themselves, a few of them internationally.

I know from experience that sometimes they may not be the best stories that these writers will create – my own 1990 story 'Tresses' now makes me more than a bit wobbly at the knees – but they are often the first stories, or the newly struck note, of a voice that will go on to new horizons. Just being short-listed for the award gives a needle-shot of confidence and a sense of breadth early in a writer's career. Publishers use it on dust-jackets. Agents take notice. And the stories, significantly, get read. And what we read is what we're yet to become.

The Hennessy Awards have been around long enough to hope that they will always be around. Kudos to the *Sunday Tribune* for keeping it alive. David Marcus has been the force behind so much of this. Ciaran Carty has given amazing depth and meaning to that force. Dermot Bolger, more than any other writer I know, has encouraged young talent and brought it through. But there's one other person to whom I owe a quiet, personal thanks. My own father, Sean McCann, was, when he worked with the *Irish Press*, instrumental in starting the New Irish Writing page – he fought for it and felt that it would last, and it has.

For that alone I would jump in another swimming pool, for that alone I still look out over rooftops. No swandive, though, just a deep bow and fall.

Colum McCann
New York
August 2005

1996

DREAMS OF SAILING

Angela Bourke

Angela Bourke was born in Dublin. She is a lecturer in Modern Irish in UCD. She writes in Irish and English and her stories have appeared in New Irish Writing, *Krino* and *Force 10*. 'Dreams of Sailing' will be published by New Island in her first collection of stories later this year. (1996)

About three weeks after I met Tony we went out to Howth and climbed up the hill with a bottle of wine instead of going to our history lecture. Tony made up a prayer to the pagan gods and before we drank the wine he poured some on the ground. He was going to be a poet. He hardly ever went to lectures. The psychiatrist in college had told him he was desperately sensitive and he was convinced all the lecturers were fools.

The wine made me dizzy. It was freezing up there, but Tony was in his element.

'*Thalassa!*' he kept saying. 'That's the Greek for sea.'

He had a big heavy coat on though.

The grass was damp and I was drunk. The sea was grey like the sky, and Tony started to talk about celebrating our love.

'Irish people have no sensuality,' he said. 'All the rain and drinking beer all the time. It'd just be sordid if we did it here.'

He thought we should wait till we got to the south of France. Under a blue pagan sky, he said. He'd never been out of Ireland and neither had I, but neither of us had ever been to bed with anyone either.

We were supposed to go to France after the exams. Normandy, then Brittany, then Paris, then on down south for the grape-picking. Tony was going to do the talking – he did French. We were going to get brown and healthy walking along dusty white roads, but then he failed his exams and went home to Waterford. To tell the truth I was relieved – he was starting to get on my nerves.

I went to Goleen instead, to stay with my aunts, and that's where I met Kevin. He was the exact opposite – big and tall and cheerful, zooming all over the place in a white Volkswagen van. His father had a hardware shop in the town and Kevin was all set to take over and expand it as soon as he finished college.

Every time I saw Kevin he was doing something. He loved being out of breath. I don't think he ever read a book. I often wonder if Bridie or Sally noticed anything, or what they thought of it all.

Bridie and Sally are my father's sisters but they're much older than he is. We were always told they weren't interested in children, so I didn't know them well. I was delighted when they asked me to stay, that they thought I was interesting enough. But there wasn't a lot to do when I got to

Goleen except walk along the cliff path. I wandered down the pier a few times but I felt self-conscious on my own, not knowing anybody.

Then Bridie said, 'Why don't you go up to the sailing club? That's where all the young people go in the evenings.'

Bridie and Sally took life so calmly. Anything they wanted to do, they just did.

And it was as simple as that. I bought myself a Harp and lime at the bar, and people talked to me. They asked me, 'What do you sail?' but there was plenty of noise and I didn't mind just standing listening. Then one of the girls said, 'Oh, there's Kevin,' and someone called him over.

He started talking to me straight away. 'I saw you down the pier yesterday, didn't I?'

Some very brown people with a lot of rings on their fingers stood near us, just back from a cruise to Brittany. They were talking about a boat called the *Sea Serpent*, and someone called Caroline who was staying on in France for a year. I think it was her boat. They kept saying things to Kevin, but he kept coming back to stand beside me, and at the end of the night he offered me a lift.

When we got to the aunts' house he sat revving the engine. I got out of the van. It wasn't that I thought he fancied me – he was just being polite to a stranger. But he leaned out the window. 'I'm trying out a Laser tomorrow afternoon if you want to come.'

Whatever a Laser was.

The next day the white van stopped beside me on the road and the door on my side opened.

'Come on. Jump in.'

I jumped in. When you've been walking around a place for days it's wonderful to get a lift.

I figured a Laser must be some kind of boat. That was

all any of them talked about. Kevin said it was really fast. He was dying to try it. It was light enough to carry on a roofrack. You could store it anywhere.

I thought of our house, with all the bikes in the hall.

It turned out a Laser was like a sailboard, only much wider. White and long and pointed and, for something lightweight, it was heavy. We loaded some of it into the van and the rest up onto the roofrack. I was amazed at all the bits and pieces. I knew about the sail and the mast, but there was the boom as well, and the rudder, and the tiller, and a thing called a daggerboard – a whole big canvas bag of things.

At the beach we did the whole operation in reverse. Kevin gave me the narrow end, but I thought I'd collapse carrying it down to the water. He went back up to the van and changed into a wetsuit. He looked hilarious but I didn't let on. He was dead serious. For someone so cheerful he didn't have much sense of humour.

I sat up in the sand-dunes with my clothes on, reading, and Kevin went over and back, over and back, in front of me. Every so often I'd look up and wave. I was reading *The French Lieutenant's Woman* so I was a bit preoccupied, but I saw him hanging out over the side once and he capsized a few times. Then I helped him drag the Laser out of the water and we did the whole business again, taking it apart and carrying it back to the van.

Driving back, Kevin looked like a big red baby, his hair all wet and plastered to his head, but he was delighted with the Laser. He said he was definitely going to buy it, only he called it 'she'.

'She's incredible, you know. She's so responsive. She really lets you feel the sea and the wind.' He wriggled his shoulders under the flannel shirt, sighing and grinning at the same time. 'That old *Sea Serpent* isn't sailing at all.'

Something made me hold my breath.

'Is that the boat that went to Brittany? Did you sail on it too?'

'I used to crew on her all the time.'

'Why didn't you go on the cruise then?'

'Well,' he said, 'myself and Caroline broke up before she went away. I thought I'd give it a miss.'

Caroline again. I imagined somebody rich and brown. A brilliant sailor. Fluent French.

'Were you and Caroline going together?' Goleen was like a photograph to me – I forgot other people had lives there before this summer.

'What? Oh yeah, for years. Sure we were living together all last year in Dublin.'

No wonder he didn't fancy me. I bet he could spot an anxious little virgin a mile away. It made me more irritated than ever about Tony.

'I'm definitely going to buy it,' Kevin said again. 'I'll tell him tonight. Would you fancy a go yourself? They can take two, you know. We could probably get hold of a wetsuit for you.'

I was so annoyed I would have said yes to anything.

So there I was the next day, wading out to meet him, with the sea seeping sneakily onto my skin through this huge wetsuit. It belonged to someone called Dave, who must have been fifteen inches broader across the shoulders than I was. I felt grotesque. Like a Martian.

I had to sit on the side and hold onto a rope. It was the sheet and that meant I was the crew. Kevin sat in the stern with the tiller and that made him the helm. All I had to do was sit there and keep hold of the rope. I was to let it out or pull it in so the sail didn't flap, and I was supposed to lean in or out to balance us.

Kevin said he'd say 'Ready about' when he was going to

turn us around and then 'Lee ho!' I was to duck under the boom when I heard that and get over to the other side without letting go of my rope. I listened in some kind of reckless despair. I had no idea how I'd got this far. I was just waiting for the rest of it to happen.

But we started off and there was nothing to it. It was like going downhill on a bike, and I began to relax. I grinned happily at Kevin and he grinned back. 'We might as well take her out in the bay.'

He pushed the tiller over a bit. I pulled the sheet in a bit and we started to go fast, out towards America. I was enjoying myself now, leaning out, getting used to the balance of it.

Then Kevin said, 'Ready about!' and 'Lee ho!' as though there was an admiral listening, instead of just me. The boom swung gently towards me and I started to do my stuff, ducking under it. But then it stuck and I saw the thing called the daggerboard sticking up, stopping it from coming any further. Everything shuddered and very slowly, yet all at once, we were in water, much lower down than before, wet and getting wetter.

I came blubbering up to the surface and Kevin was on the other side of the boat, laughing. This was something I was supposed to take in my stride. Part of the fun, but I wasn't doing it right. My nose was running and my mouth was full of the sea. I had thick rubber sponge all over my body, along with a lifejacket. I couldn't swim – I was crawling on top of the water like an insect. There was nowhere I could go. The Laser was face down in the water and the land was miles away.

Kevin was paddling around over there, turning the upside-down boat into the wind, being efficient. I hung in the water, deciding to trust him. At least he knew about capsizes. I was getting used to the feel of my lifejacket – like an armchair in the water. The people in the clubhouse probably did this all the time.

Kevin managed to do something with his feet. He shouted across to me and up she came.

The mast and the sail came swinging up against the blue sky, with the sun shining on all the drops of water as they poured off. It looked so beautiful and geometric, very high and white and far away. I was beginning to understand why people love sailing so much, even the falling in, when something crashed onto my head.

It was the mast. The top of the mast. I was miles away from it, but it was long. If I'd been standing on concrete instead of on water it would have split my skull. At first I thought it had. It hurt like anything.

'Kevin!' I yelled, and his red face grinned back at me between the waves, further and further away. I kept expecting to lose consciousness. The thing I had on was a buoyancy aid, not a lifejacket: I'd be floating face down in the water.

'I'm hurt, for Christ's sake! I can't do anything!'

I kept swallowing water, but finally he got the boat up again and it stayed up. He brought it to where I was and hauled me on. Carefully, we made it back to the beach.

Kevin was smiling again by the time we got there. 'That was great, wasn't it?'

I didn't say anything, but it didn't matter.

He dropped me off at my aunts' house. 'I'll see you tonight then.'

By the time I'd had a bath and washed my hair I felt okay. Bridie and Sally were both out. I was aching all over, but I was dry, and going up to the club in the evening I felt I'd had my initiation.

Kevin seemed to think so too. He stood with his arm

around me, talking to a man called Bill who'd just bought an oyster bed. Someone mentioned Caroline and I realised Bill was her father. He looked very young.

When closing time came, we walked out to the van together and I got in my side.

Kevin drove by the coast road instead of straight down to the village, and when we came to the lay-by near the cliff path he stopped the van. He said we might as well go for a walk, so of course we did, and of course he put his arms around me and we kissed on the cliff path. We walked back up to the van.

'That was a scream today, wasn't it?' he said. He held me against the side of the van. The nights are very short that time of year. There was a lot of blue in the sky over his shoulder.

'You know, when I saw you down on the pier with your book I thought you were a real snooty intellectual, but you have a lovely pair of tits.'

I was glad my face was against his shoulder so he couldn't see it.

The next thing he said was, 'I want to make love to you,' and he started kissing me again.

'So this is it, is it?'

I haven't any sisters but sometimes I imagine one, younger than me and a bit cynical. That was her voice inside my head.

'I never thought it'd happen this soon,' I muttered to her. 'I have to do it sometime.'

She grinned at me and shrugged.

Kevin opened the back of the van. There was a piece of carpet on the floor. It hadn't been there that afternoon.

'Come on,' he said.

It didn't take very long and it hurt like hell, and after it was over he handed me a box of tissues. They hadn't been there in the afternoon either. At least it was dark in there. We got back into the front seats and he drove me home. He didn't say anything. I thought it was because I was a virgin. I thought he was disgusted or disappointed or something, but he gave me a quick, absent-minded sort of a kiss. 'You'd better go in. See you tomorrow.'

I was there another six days, and every day Kevin picked me up at the harbour. We drove to the beach and I helped him get the Laser off the roofrack and carry it down to the water. We assembled the mast and the boom and I held the sail while he fed the mast into the sleeve along the side. Then I'd lie in the sun or sit in the sand-dunes with my book and after a while he'd come back, all dripping and exhilarated, and ask me if I'd seen this or that, and I'd go and help him haul the boat out of the water. Every evening we went to the club and every night Kevin drove me home the long way. We stopped in the lay-by on the cliff road and made love in the back of the van. I couldn't honestly say I enjoyed it, but I did learn a lot. It turned out he'd never done it with Caroline, even though they'd shared a flat. 'We had plenty of sex,' he said, a bit grumpy when I asked him. 'We just never made love.'

I nearly laughed, but he was serious. 'Caroline wants to keep her virginity till she gets married,' he said. 'I respect that.'

He didn't seem to care if I just lay there, so I was able to think about the whole business. I thought about Tony, with his poetry and his bottles of wine, and Kevin with his heaving and grunting. I thought of all the kinds of people there must be in between, and about the way I'd like to do it if I got a chance. Maybe I would get a chance, now the hard part was over.

I got a lot of reading done in those six days. I finished *The French Lieutenant's Woman* and went on to three or four Jane

Austens that were in Bridie and Sally's. I didn't fancy another attempt at sailing. Kevin was still all excited about the Laser, but it was really only made for one person.

Angela Bourke's first short story collection, *By Salt Water*, was published by New Island in 1996. In 2001 she received *The Irish Times* Irish Literature Prize for Non-Fiction for *The Burning of Bridget Cleary* (London, Pimlico, 2000). She was joint editor of *The Field Day Anthology*, vols 4 and 5, *Irish Women's Writing and Traditions* (Cork, Cork University Press, 2002). Her most recent book is a cultural biography, *Maeve Brennan: Homesick at* The New Yorker (London, Pimlico, 2005).

WHERE THE WATER'S DEEPEST

Claire Keegan

Claire Keegan is 27. She was a runner-up in
the 1995 Francis MacManus Award and has
received several other awards. She has taught
creative writing and was, until recently, Writer
in Residence in Virginia House, Tallaght. She
now lives in Westmeath. (1996)

The au pair sits on the edge of the
pier this night, fishing. Beside
her, cheese she salvaged from the
salad bowl at dinner, her leather san-
dals. She removes the band from her
ponytail and shakes her hair loose.
Leftover smells of cooking and bath-
suds drift down from the house
through the trees. She slides a cube of
cheese onto the hook and casts. Her
wrist is good. The line makes a perfect arc, drops down and vanishes.
Slowly she reels it towards her, where
the water's deepest. She's caught a
nice perch this way before.

Lately she's not been sleeping

well, wakes to the same dream. She and the boy are in the yard at evening time. Wind bloats the clothes on the line and black trees are nuzzling overhead. Then the ground trembles. Stars drop and jingle around their feet like coins. The barn roof shudders, lifts off like a great metal leaf, scraping clouds. The earth fractures open and the boy is left standing on the other side.

'Jump! Jump, I'll catch you!' she yells.

The boy is smiling. He trusts her.

'Come on!' she holds her arms open wide. 'Jump! It's easy!'

He runs fast and jumps. His feet clear the canyon but then the strangest thing happens: her hands melt and the boy drops backwards into the darkness. The au pair just stands on the edge and watches him fall.

Sometimes she dreams this twice in the same night. Last night she got up and smoked a cigarette in the bathroom and watched the moon. The light slid off the gold-plated taps, dipped into the porcelain sink, making shadow. She brushed her teeth and went back to bed.

That afternoon they'd dug up worms and carried their fishing gear down to the lakeshore. The au pair flipped the boat right-side-up and slid it into the water, held it steady for the boy. 'Right-ho!' she said and rowed them out past the shade of the pier. The boy was wearing a Salt Lake City baseball cap his father brought back from a business trip. Freckles had grown together across his nose; the scab on his knee was healing. His hand dangled over the side and tore the water's surface as she rowed. When she raised the oars they drifted into a black cloud of mosquitoes.

'Do they have bugs in the Reef?' the boy asked.

The au pair's voice changed when she talked about home. She talked as if she could reach out through the past

and touch it with her hands. She baited his hook, told him
how she'd learned to scuba dive and snorkel with a spear,
explored the hidden world under the ocean. Gigantic
mountains where the fish swam in schools and changed
direction all at once. Seaweed swirling. A turtle with great
spirals on his back, swimming past. Seahorses.

'I wanna go scuba-diving here,' the boy said.

'We can't, love. Your lake's too dark and muddy. The
bottom isn't sandy like the ocean – it's deep mud, deeper
than two grown men standing on top of each other. Way
too dangerous for diving.'

The boy turned quiet for a while. Quarter horses in the
far meadow whinnied and cantered down the hill, snorted to
a stop at the water's edge.

'Let's play what's it like!' she said and slapped a bug on
her arm.

The boy shrugged. 'Okay.'

She took the first turn: 'This boat is like one half of a
big brazil nut.'

'Your head is like a cabbage.'

'Your eyelashes are the colour of a palomino's mane.'

'What's that?' the boy asked.

'A type of horse. I'll show you a picture sometime.'

'I've eyes like a horse?'

'Your turn.'

'Your farts are like baked beans.'

'Your farts are like deadly silences,' she said.

'You're like a Mama,' he said, and looked into her eyes.

'Speaking of Mamas,' she said, 'your Mama should be
home soon. We better get on home.' She gripped the oars
and rowed them back to shore.

Before dinner they sat on rugs in the den and made cards
out of thick, expensive paper his Mama bought downtown
and called each other partners: 'Merry Easter, Partner. Eat

lotsa eggs,' his card read. She held his hand, wrote the letters for him, but he told her what to write. He drew the X's on the bottom by himself. On the front, in crayon, he drew two stick figures on a brown background.

'What are those?' his father asked. A big, red-haired man with Irish ancestors and eyes an unrelenting shade of blue. He was smoking a cigar, watching CNN with his feet up.

'Scuba divers,' the boy said.

'I see,' he said. 'Come here, son.'

The boy rose and climbed up on his father's lap.

'Take a break, sweetheart,' the man told the au pair.

She got up. She passed the dishes in the kitchen sink, walked out into the night and slammed the door.

Down at the lake the au pair hears the toilet flush, then the swash of bathwater in the pipes. Bedtime. The boy's Mama, a tall, blonde woman with high cheekbones who runs a real-estate agency downtown, always puts the boy to bed. That is the arrangement. She bathes the boy, reads *Green Eggs and Ham* or *Where the Wild Things Are*. His Mama is well educated. Sometimes she reads from a book of poems by Robert Frost and plays Mozart on the stereo. Later, the au pair will go in and see if the boy is still awake; she will turn the night-light on in the bathroom and kiss him good-night.

Last winter they travelled north, a three hour flight to New York City for a long weekend. They stayed in a hotel suite nineteen floors up with a small balcony and a view of Manhattan. That evening the boy's Mama dressed up in a loose silk dress and a mink jacket, took her husband's arm and they went out to dinner. The au pair ordered pizza funghi and Coca-Colas from room-service, played snakes and ladders with the boy. He threw the dice and they climbed and slithered up and down the board till bedtime.

The au pair stayed up, took a hot shower and wrapped herself in the fluffy dressing gown with the Hilton crest impressed on the lapel. She opened the balcony door and, from the armchair, watched the skyline, the evening bleeding into darkness behind the tallest buildings, but she didn't dare go out and look down. Instead she wrote letters home, saying she might not be back for Christmas after all, how she missed the ocean but they were good to her, she wanted for nothing.

It was late when they got back. She'd dozed off in the chair, but woke to hear them talking in the bedroom. Then the talking stopped and the man went out on the balcony. Cigar smoke and freezing cold air drifted back into the room. He bolted the balcony doors and came back in and sat on the edge of the couch looking down at her. He smelled of vodka and Polo aftershave and the au pair felt the cold off his good wool suit.

'You know what happens if we lose the baby, don't you?' he said. 'We lose the baby, we lose a baby-sitter. You keep those balcony doors locked, sweetheart, or you'll be taking the first plane home.' He kissed her then, a strange, deliberate kiss, an airport kiss for someone you're glad to see the back of, then got up and went back into his wife.

When she heard his snores, she rose and stepped out on the balcony. A weak wind was driving large snowflakes across the air, sifting them into flurries. It was a December night speckled with snow and the hooting of traffic. Soon it would be Christmas. She gripped the railings and looked down. A snarl of angry, yellow taxis clotted the intersections on the streets below. She sucked her breath in. She remembered reading somewhere that a fear of heights masks an attraction to falling. Suddenly, that made some kind of terrifying sense to her. If she didn't think of jumping off, standing on the edge wouldn't matter. She imagined falling, imagined how that might feel, to dive down, be lost like that, to mean everything for moments only, then be gone, the relief of having everything over and done with. Then she backed inside and locked the doors.

The next morning they planned to visit F.A.O. Schwarz Toystore. In the lobby, the au pair wrote the boy's name and his room number on a slip of paper and pinned it to the inside of his trouser pocket.

'Now give this to the nearest policeman if you get lost.'

'But I won't get lost!' he said.

'Of course you won't.'

It is dark now down at the lake. The au pair senses movement in the bushes at the far bank. Somewhere in those fields are wild boars. Once the boy's father trapped a boar, paid a man to slaughter the animal and stacked the deep-freeze solid. Another dozen casts or so and she'll turn in. The cheese is nearly used up anyhow. She listens to the frogs ribbuting and for some reason remembers the tock, tock of the electric fence back home. Her father taught her never to touch it with the palm, always the back of the hand – that way the reflex would make her pull away, not grip it if the current was still running. Small things, that's what fathers are for, far as she can see. How to tie your shoelaces and buckle your seat-belt. She reels in the line and checks the bait, casts again. The bait plops but she can no longer detect the line against the sky.

Nobody sees the boy leave the house. He sneaks down the back steps but doesn't hold onto the railing like he's told. It doesn't matter that his eyes have not adjusted to the darkness; he knows the grassy slope that leads down to the lake. He can see her pale blouse, the sleeve coming up, the elbow whipping back, casting. The boy runs although he is told never to run near water. Small grunts, like the noises his cousin's doll makes when he turns her upside-down and right-side-up again, come from his chest. The au pair has her back to him. The boy's feet are soundless; he is silent as a panther in the cool grass.

The au pair doesn't turn her head until his foot hits the first plank of the pier.

'Yoo-hoo! Catch me! Catch me!' the boy calls.

He is running, fast. The rod drops from her hands. The boy's foot catches on something and then he seems to travel a long, long way. The au pair is finding her feet, trying to stand and turn all at once. The boy feels a chill. Suddenly her arms are there, enfolding him as he knew they would. He flops down and giggles on her shoulder.

'Surprise!' he yells.

But she isn't laughing.

The boy goes silent. Beyond the safety of her shoulder, he detects danger. Beyond her, there is nothing. Only deep water and mud deeper than two grown men.

'Oh, my baby,' the au pair whispers. 'There, there.'

She rocks him and rests his head on her shoulder for a long time, feeling his chest fall and rise. She kisses the silk of his hair; his eyelashes brush against her collarbone. The au pair holds him until their heartbeats slow and a woman's voice calls out the boy's name. Then she carries him back up to the lighted house and gives him to his Mama.

Claire Keegan's collection of stories, *Antarctica* (Faber & Faber), won the Francis MacManus Award, The Kilkenny Prize, The Macaulay Fellowship, The Martin Healy Award, The William Trevor Prize, The Olive Cook Award and the Rooney Prize for Irish Literature. She has also received awards from The Arts Council, The Royal Society of Authors and The Harold Hyam Wingate Foundation. She now lives and works in Cork, where she is writer in residence at UCC.

1997

'Yes. When they were home this summer, the night before they went back to England.'

He stopped a moment, still half-stooped over the range. He opened his mouth, then closed it again, making no sound, like a goldfish in a bowl. He tried again and, still choked with emotion, managed a broken sentence:

'And your mother – did she know?'

'Dunno,' I said. 'Mothers know a lot more than they get told.'

'They do, they do. God rest them.' He blessed himself, awkwardly. 'But fathers know nothing. Nothing until it's spelt out for them.'

He was standing at the table filling an already full kettle with well-water from the bucket. He placed it on the range again as if he was making tea the way he did after milking-time. He always made tea with well-water, boiling it in the old kettle instead of using tap-water and the electric kettle, unless it was early in the morning when he'd no time. It would save on the electric, he said. Even mum couldn't get him to change. She wanted rid of the range altogether since the electric cooker was more consistent, more dependable for everything – dinners, cooking, boiling, baking, heating milk for the calves … There's always the chance of a power-cut, he'd say whenever there was a storm or thunder. If the electric runs out, it'll come in handy. And any time it happened, he'd turn to us, delighted, and say, 'Aren't you glad now of the old range?'

He lifted the poker. Opened the top door of the range. Plunged it in to stir up the fire, trying to draw some flames from the depths. When the embers didn't respond very well, he turned the knob at the top of the range somewhat clumsily, making the chimney suck up the flame. He poked the fire another couple of times, a bit deeper, trying to let the air through. Soon there were flames dancing, blue and red, licking the dark sods and fizzing and flitting over the hard

FATHER

Micheál Ó Conghaile

Micheál Ó Conghaile, a Connemara writer and publisher, was born in 1962. He is from Inis Treabhair originally, but now living in Indreabhán, Co. Galway. His account of the social history of Connemara, *Conamara & Árainn 1890–1980: Gnéithe den Stair Shóisialta*, won an Irish Book Award in 1988. His first short story collection, *Mac an tSagairt*, was published in 1986 and his first poetry collection, *Combrá Cailif*, was published in 1987. He established the publishing company Cló Iar-Chonnachta (CIC) in 1985 and the company has since published over 300 books and 200 traditional Irish music albums and spoken word albums to date. This is his first published work in English. (1997)

How was I supposed to know what to do – once I'd told him? I'd never seen my da crying before. Even when mum died nine months ago in the accident he never cried, as far as I know. I'm sure of it because it was I brought him the bad news.

And I was around the whole time, up to and after the funeral. It was my job to stay with him. His brothers and my mother's brothers – my uncles – made all the arrangements, shouldered the coffin. And it was the neighbours, instructed by my sisters, who kept the house in some order. There was a sort of an understanding – unspoken, mind you – that it was best I stay with dad since I was the youngest, the only one still at home all year round.

That's how I'm nearly sure he didn't shed a tear. Not in the daylight hours anyway. He didn't need his hanky even. Sure, he was all over the place – you could hardly get a word out of him. Long silences would go by and he just stared into the fire or out the kitchen window. But no tears. Maybe it was the shock. The terrible shock to his system. But then again, you wouldn't really associate tears or crying with my father.

That's why I was so taken aback. Mortified. Not just the crying. But the way he cried. In fact, you couldn't really call it crying – it was more like something between a groan and a sob stuck in his throat. Yes, a muffled, pained sigh of revulsion a few seconds long. You'd've thought he choked on it like one of those horrible pills the doctor gives you. And he didn't even look at me, except for a stray watery glance that skirred by when I told him; afterwards, it was like he was trying to hide his face from me, half of it anyway. It should've been easier for him in a way; but not for me, there was no way I could look him in the face, for all my curiosity. So, while he dithered about, I sat there like a statue – only for my body-heat. The breath was knocked out of him, and me. Then I realised that even his smothered cry – if it could be let out – was better than this silence. Maybe you could do something about the cry, if it happened. A deadly silence was unworkable, impossible, as long drawn-out and painful as a judgment. I felt all the time that he wasn't looking anywhere near me, even when he got his breath back and some speech.

'And you …' he said, as if the word stuck or swelled up in his throat until he didn't know if it was safe to release it or rather he hoped, perhaps, that I would say it – the word that had popped in his ears just now, a word he was never likely to form in his rural throat unless it was spat out in some smutty joke for the lads down the pub. A word there wasn't even a word for in Irish, not easy to find anyway … I forgot I hadn't answered him, carried away trying to read his mind when suddenly he repeated:

'Are you telling me you're …'

'Yes,' I said, half-consciously interrupting him with the same reticence, unsure whether he was going to finish his sentence this time, or not.

'I am,' I said again quickly, uncontrollably, trying for a moment to make up for the empty silence.

'God save us,' he said. 'God *save* us,' he said again as if he had to drag the words individually all the way from Mexico. It seemed to me he wanted to say more, anything, an answer or just some ready-made platitude, a string of words to pluck from the silence.

'Do you see that now?' he complained, taking a deep sniff of the kitchen air and blowing it out again with force. 'Do you see that now?'

He grabbed the coal-bucket and opened the range to top up the fire. Then he lifted a couple of bits of turf out of the 10-10-20 plastic bag beside the range and – breaking the last two bits in half over his knee to build up his corner of the crammed space of the open range – shoved them on top. The coal was too hot – and too dear, he'd say – plus it was hard to burn the turf sometimes, or get much heat out of it, especially if it was still a bit soggy after a bad summer. He took the handbrush off the hook and swept any powdery bits of turf on the range into the fire. He slid the curly iron frame back into place with a clatter and took another deep breath, focusing on the range.

'And have you told your sisters about this?'

coal, shyly at first but growing in courage and strength. He closed the door with a deep thud, turning the knob firmly with his left hand, and put the poker back in the corner.

'And what about Síle Jimí Beag?' he asked suddenly, as if surprised he hadn't asked about her earlier. 'Weren't you going out with her a few years ago?' he said, a hint of hope rising in his voice.

'Yes ... in a way,' I stammered. I knew that was no answer but it was the best I could do just then.

'In a way,' he repeated. 'What do you mean? You were or you weren't. Wasn't she coming here for a year and God knows how long before that? Didn't she leave Tomáisín Tom Mhary for you?' He stared at the bars over the range.

'But I was only ... only eighteen back then,' I said, changing my mind. 'Nobody knows what they want at that age, or where they're going,' I added.

'But they do at twenty-two, it seems! They think they know it all at twenty-two.'

'It's not that simple, really,' I said, surprising myself at going so far.

'Oh, sure, it's not simple. It's anything but!'

He pushed the kettle aside and opened the top of the range again as if he was checking to see the fire was still lit. It was.

'I went out with her, because I didn't know — I didn't know what to do, because all the other lads had a girl ...'

'Oh, you were ...'

'I asked her in the first place because I had to take somebody to the school formal. Everyone was taking some girl or other. I couldn't go alone. And it would've been odd to take Máirín or Eilín. They wouldn't have gone anyway. I couldn't stay at home because I'd've been the only one in my class not there. What else could I do?' I said, amazed I'd managed to get that much out.

'How do I know what you should've done? Couldn't you

just be like everyone else … that, that or stay home?' There was something about the way he said 'home'.

'I couldn't,' I said, 'not forever … It's not that I didn't try …' I thought it best to go no further, afraid he wouldn't understand.

'So that's what brings you up to Dublin so much,' he said, glad to have worked that much out for himself.

'Yes. Yes, I suppose.' What else could I say, I thought.

'And we were all convinced you had a woman up there. People asking me if we'd met her yet, or when we'd get to see her. Aunty Nóra asking just the other day when we'd have the next wedding, thinking a year after your mother's death would be OK.'

'Aunty Nóra doesn't have to worry about me. It's as well she didn't get married herself anyway,' I said, scunnered as soon as I'd said it at the suggestion I was making.

'Up to Dublin! Huh.' He spoke to himself. 'Dublin's quare and dangerous,' he added, in a way that didn't require an answer.

He turned around, his back to the range. Clambered over to the kitchen table. Tilted the milk-cooler with his two hands to pour a drop of it into the jug till it was near overflowing. I was glad he never spilt any on the table, ready to clean it up if I had to. I felt awkward and ashamed sitting there watching him do this – my job usually. He poured the extra milk that wouldn't fit in the jug into the saucepan the calves used and set it on the side of the range to heat it up until the cows were milked; after that he'd see to the calves. He lifted the enamel milk-bucket that was always set on the table-rails once it was cleaned every morning after the milking. Then he gave it a good scalding with hot water from the kettle – water boiled stupid that had the kettle singing earlier. He set down the kettle, with its mouth turned in, back on the side of the range so that it wouldn't boil over with the heat. He swirled the scalding water around the bottom of the bucket and then emptied it in one go into the calves' saucepan. He stretched over a bit to grab the dishcloth off the rack above the range. Dried the bucket. Hung it up again rather carelessly, watching to see it didn't roll down on top of the range. It didn't.

All at once, he straightened up as if a thought had suddenly struck him. He turned round to me. Looked for a second as our eyes met and went over each other. The look he gave was different from the first — that soft sudden glance he gave me when I first told him. I noticed the wrinkles across his forehead, some curled, some squared off, the short grey hair pulled down in a fringe, the eyebrows, the eyes. What eyes! It was those eyes drove out of me whatever dream was going through my head just then. Those eyes caught me out all right. Those eyes that could say so much without him even having to open his mouth. I understood then that the only way to look at a man was right in the eyes, even if it was a casual side-glance, on the sly ... I looked away, couldn't take any more, grateful that he took it upon himself to speak. He had the bucket tucked up under his armpit the way he did when he was going out milking.

'And what about your health?' he managed to say, nervously. 'Is your health OK?'

'Oh, I'm fine, just fine,' I replied quick as I could, more than glad to be able to give such a clear answer. I started tapping my fingers. Then it struck me just what he was asking.

'God preserve us from the like of that,' he said over his shoulder to me, on his way to the door. You could tell he was relieved.

'You don't have to worry,' I said, trying to build his trust, having got that far. 'I'm careful. Very careful. Always.'

'Can you be a hundred per cent careful?' he added

curiously, his voice more normal. 'I mean if half what's in the Sunday papers and the week's TV is true.'

I let him talk away, realising he probably knew much more than I thought. Wasn't the TV always turned towards him, with all sorts of talk going on in some of the programmes while he sat there in the big chair with his eyes closed, dozing by the fire it seemed but probably taking it all in.

He took his coat down off the back of the door, set it over the chair.

'And did you have to tell me all this at my age?'

'Yes and no.' I'd said it before I realised, but I continued: 'Well, I'm not saying I had to, but I was afraid you'd hear it from someone else, afraid someone'd say something about me with you there.' I thought I was getting through. 'I thought you should know anyway; I thought you were ready.'

'Ready! I'm ready now all right ... And are you telling me people round here know?' he said, disgusted.

'Yes, as it happens. You can't hide anything, especially in a remote place like this.'

'And you think you can stay around here?' he exclaimed in what sounded to me like horror. His words hit home so quick I didn't know whether they were meant as a statement or a question. Did they require an answer, from me or himself, I wondered. Sure, I was intending to stay, or I should say, happy to stay. He was my father. I was the youngest, the only son. My two sisters had emigrated. It was down to me. Although my sisters had convinced me the night before they went away that there was always a place for me in London if I needed it.

Surely, he should've known I would want to stay. Who else would look out for him? Help with the few animals we had, look after the house, keep an eye on our wee bit of a farm, see he was all right, take him to Mass on Sunday, keep him company ... 'And you think you can stay around here.'

I wondered, none the wiser, still trying to work out whether I was to take it as a question or a statement; if he expected an answer or not.

He'd dragged his wellingtons over between the chair and the head of the table and was bent down struggling to undo the laces of his hobnailed boots. He looked different that way. If I had to go, I said to myself ... If he threw me out and told me he didn't want to see me or have anything more to do with me ...

Right away, I recalled some of my mates and acquaintances in Dublin. The ones that were kicked out by their families when they found out: Mark whose father called him a dirty bastard and told him not to come near the house again as long as he lived; Keith whose da gave him a bad beating when he discovered he'd a lover, and who kept him locked up at home for a month even though he was near twenty; Philip who was under so much stress he'd a nervous breakdown, who'd no option but to leave his teaching job after one of his worst pupils saw him leaving a particular Sunday-night venue and the news spread by lunch-time the following Monday. The boys called him disgusting names right to his face, never mind the unconcealed whispers behind his back. Who could blame him for leaving, even if it meant the dole and finding a new flat across town? The dole didn't even come into it for Robin ... Twenty-four hours his parents gave him to clear out of the house and take all he had with him, telling him he wasn't their son, that he'd brought all this on himself, that they never wanted to see him again as long as he lived. Which they didn't. Coming home that night to find his body laid out on the bed in their room, empty pillboxes on his chest, half a glass of water under the mirror on the dressing-table, a short crumpled note telling them that his only wish was to die where he was born, that he loved them, and was sorry he hurt them but saw no other way.

The slow-rolling chimes of the clock interrupted my litany. He was still opposite me, working away trying to pull on his boots with great difficulty, his trousers tucked down his thick woollen socks. If I had to go, I thought, I'd never see my father like this again. Never. The next time I'd see him, he'd be stone-cold dead in his coffin, the three of us back together on the first plane from London after getting an urgent phone call from home telling us he was found slumped in the garden, or that they weren't sure if he fell in the fire or was dead before the fire burnt the house to the ground overnight, or maybe they'd find him half-dressed in the bedroom after some of the neighbours forced in the door, trying to work out when was the last time they saw him, no one able to work out exactly the time of death ...

He'd got into his wellingtons and stood there wrapped up in his great coat, holding his cap, about to put it on, the enamel milk-bucket under his arm.

He moved slowly, tottered almost, over to the front door. My eyes followed his face, his side, his back, his awkward steps away from me as his last words of a moment ago went round and round in my head like an eel scooped out of a well on a hot summer day and set on a warm stone.

He paused at the door the way he always did on his way out and dunked his finger in the holy-water font hung up on the door jamb. It was an old wooden font with the Sacred Heart on it that my mother brought back from a pilgrimage to Knock the time the Pope was over. I could see him trying to bless himself, not even sure if it was the finger or thumb he'd dipped in the holy water he was using.

He placed his hand on the latch. Opened it and pulled it towards him.

He turned round and looked at me, head first, his body following slowly. He was staring right at me, which stopped my mind racing and swept my thoughts back to their dark corners.

'Will you stand by the braddy* cow for me?' he asked, 'while I'm milking ... she's always had a sore teat ...'

* Irish *bradach*: thieving, trespassing
translated by Frank Sewell

Micheál Ó Conghaile was elected to Aosdána in 1998. His first novel, *Sna Fir (Among Men)*, was published in 1999, and was short-listed for *The Irish Times* Literature Awards 2001. He has translated Martin McDonagh's plays into Irish and his works have been translated into various languages. His third collection of short stories, *An Fear Nach nDéanann Gáire (The Man Who Never Laughs)* was published in July 2003 and his first play, *Cúigear Chonamara*, was awarded the Stewart Parker/BBC Ulster Award and an Oireachtas Award. The English translation, *The Connemara Five*, is published by Arlen House.

1998

FLINT

Philip Ó Ceallaigh

Originally from Waterford, Philip Ó
Ceallaigh has lived and worked in Spain,
Russia, the US and Romania and now lives
in Galway. (1998)

Andrea, Laura and Patti were arm-in-arm, singing, walking to the
Back Room Bar. The song burst out
of them from happiness because it
was Saturday night, summertime and
they were full of wine. Andrea, singing with raucous abandon, head
thrown back, was the tallest. A loose
T-shirt and jeans buckled low around
her hips showed a deliberate attempt
to hide her form. Patty was short and
plump and her frizzy hair formed a
halo. Her tiny eyes were lost behind
thick glasses and her voice was
quavering and uncertain.

Laura, intermediate in height,
held them together and filled harmo-
niously the gaps between the voices
of her friends. Her soft brown hair

fell around her shoulders and although there was a touch of tiredness around her eyes the beginning of a smile lit her face. The song was an old one called 'My Girl'. It asked 'What can make me feel this way?' and just as the chorus was bouncing back with an enthusiastic 'My girl!' Ray stumbled out of the Back Room, breaking their harmony and knocking them apart.

'What the fuck?'

'Asshole!'

He shambled across the alley and beat the roof of his car with his fists, shouting 'fuck' many times, then got into the car and reversed into a row of trash cans. Tyres screeched and he barely slowed as he took the left towards Saginaw.

At the far end of the bar came the discordant sounds of a heavy metal band tuning up. They had not yet seen what the three friends saw as they entered. Angie was slumped across the stairs up to the pool room, blood running from her mouth and head. Larry the barman, wiping his fingers on his pants, came out from behind the counter. Laura was already helping her to her feet.

'She's drunk. They were drinking for hours. She was baiting him. Then he slaps her one in the mouth and runs out.'

The blood poured from a cut inside the mouth where the teeth had sliced the lip and from a cut on the side of her head where she had fallen against the stairs.

'Aren't you going to notify the police?' Andrea demanded.

Larry shrugged. 'She's the one who has to press charges.' He sauntered back behind the bar. 'Not the first time he's slapped her. Her boyfriend is a prick. Why doesn't she dump him? I just work here y'know. Maybe if God had checked things out with me before he made the world I could have suggested some improvements. I feel sorry for her and everything, but what can I do? Adopt her?'

The three friends glared at him.

'Shut up, Larry,' said Laura. 'Give me a cloth for her head. A clean one.'

Larry threw her one. 'Hey, don't give me a hard time. Jesus, people are always coming in here with all their problems, getting into fights, puking up around the place, getting fucked up, and then their friends come in and dump on me because I'm not a fucking social worker. If I could, I'd ban the stuff like the Arabians do. Can't see that it does any of you any good.'

Zak, Laura's boyfriend, entered. He was not tall but he was well-built. He looked older than Laura, though they were both in their late twenties. Fine lines radiated from his sharp blue eyes as if he had been a long time squinting into the sun, and his hair was flecked with grey above the ears. Laura explained what had happened as she and Patti helped Angie – drunk and bloody – to her feet. They would take her to hospital as she probably needed some stitches.

'Listen,' said Zak, 'I can go with you, but my shift starts in an hour and, you know, you could take longer than that.'

'Sure, there's no point you coming. We'll take care of her.'

What Zak said made sense. From midnight to seven a.m. he manned a gas station kiosk. There was no reason, Laura told herself, why she should feel resentment, as if he were somehow to blame for this mess of a Saturday night. Yet resentment was there. Laura and Andrea helped Angie out of the bar. Angie held the cloth to her head to control the bleeding. Laura looked back as the door swung closed. With one hand Larry placed a bottle of beer in front of Zak and with the other he began to wipe the counter. The girls stepped over the refuse from the overturned trashcans in the alley.

Driving past the lights of the strip their silent watchful faces passed in and out of illumination. Past the malls and stores and warehouses stranded in vast lots like the hulks of abandoned ships. Past Burger King and Taco Bell, screaming their special offers, fluorescent in the night though locked up and empty of human life. There was not a soul to be seen anywhere along the strip, as though the population had vanished and left only its junk to be remembered by; a few factories, pylons, phone lines, traffic lights, billboards and useless neon signs, high on their pedestals, winking, signalling to nobody.

They drove past a windowless bar, vast and squat and featureless like a concrete bunker. GIRLS GIRLS GIRLS announced the flashing light. Another said LIVE DAN-CING GIRLS and another, further on, FLOOR SHOW. And still not a soul, only parked cars and pick-up trucks. Laura turned on the radio to drive away the silence but all she could get was static, then two voices, distant and crackling as if coming down from the vast black spaces between the stars, cutting over each other so that neither could be heard, then an electric whine that coalesced into the voice of a preacher who warned of eternal damnation and prophesied the destruction of the cities of the plain, then a country tune with a lazy beat like the dismal clip-clopping of a pony's hooves on concrete. The tuner moved back into static.

'The rest doesn't work,' she said, and turned it off.

The doctor, a brisk, fresh-smelling young man, assessed the damage.

'Hm, lip is fine. The bruising looks unpleasant, but lips and gums heal rapidly. Disinfect your mouth regularly over the next few days.' He held an eyelid open and shone a pencil torch into the pupil. 'Doesn't appear to be any concussion. Nasty gash, though. That'll require stitches.' An X-ray showed that there was no deeper damage. The doctor explained to Laura that Angie should spend the night in hospital. It was standard procedure for head injuries. She could call for someone to pick her up in the morning.

Angie was given a room to herself with a tiny window. They all went up to say goodnight to her. Her face was drawn but she had sobered up considerably and she looked better in her hospital gown than in her bloodstained T-shirt.

'I want you to tell him,' said Angie, her voice tremulous with tears and anger. 'Tell that bastard he's put me in the hospital this time.'

'Oh, Angie, what's the point even talking to him?' said Laura.

'I'll call him,' said Andrea. 'I'll tell him.'

'Promise?'

'I said I'd call him, didn't I?'

'Is it going to leave a scar?' asked Angie, pathetically.

'It's behind your hairline,' said Patti. 'Nobody will see.'

'Jesus Christ, you straight bitches,' snorted Andrea. 'A man nearly knocks your brains out and you worry if you're still pretty.'

They laughed. Angie's smile turned to a grimace. Her lip was too sore. Andrea put her arm around her. 'You don't need him. You don't need any of them.'

'Listen, Angie,' said Laura, taking her hand. 'I've a spare room. You can stay with me until you're sorted out.'

'Yeah,' said Patti. 'We'll go get your things out of there tomorrow. You won't even have to talk to him.

'This is the best thing that ever happened to you,' said Andrea. 'You'll see.'

Angie smiled with the good half of her mouth. Her chin wrinkled up, her lips trembled and tears welled between her puffy red eyelids.

'You guys are great. No, I mean it, you're the best.'

Andrea told her to cut it out. Laura told her she needed to sleep, to call her in the morning. They hugged her in turn.

Outside, Patti asked Andrea if she was really going to call Ray.

'You must be kidding. I'm not going to call that cocksucker.'

After leaving the hospital they went for something to eat, then smoked some dope and watched the sun rise over the Flint river at a place where they had played when they were children. It was after six when Laura arrived home. In little over an hour Zak would be home, so she decided to stay awake and wait for him. The cat pawed the window. It rubbed itself against her when she let it in and begged to be fed.

Zak. He never looked beyond the world he knew, never questioned, never wanted new places, as if he had been born complete and so without curiosity. Laura had been unable to tolerate this when she was younger. Though she liked his steadiness and reliability, a day came when she wanted to make her life in a new place, with new people. She told him they had grown apart. He had just nodded.

'Well,' he said, 'if you need me you know where to find me,' and touched her cheek. It had made her angry at the time that this was his only response.

After two years in New York she returned home, admitting to nobody her sense of failure. New York had been exciting. She had had good jobs, known men, lived the things she was supposed to live, and got tired of it all. Her best friend had returned to her home town after nearly dying of an overdose. Laura decided she needed a rest too.

But returning home wasn't as she had expected either. Nobody was very much interested in what had happened to her, except in the most transient, conversational way. People had their own personal dramas, rising and subsiding and being forgotten on the tide of everyday life. It was as though she had never left at all and her struggle had counted for nothing.

When she called to Zak's house he was sitting at the

kitchen table with his brothers, the dinner things before them. The scene was just as they had left it two years before. Moths bumped blindly against the screen door. They walked in the dark through the neighbourhood and the same domestic sounds came echoing across the yards from the open windows of the houses and glimpses of life could be caught in the bright lighted squares. She had no way to speak of the things that had happened to her, while he talked easily about people they both knew in the town, about things he was doing, about maybe renting a cabin on Lake Michigan with some friends. It would be nice to get away from Flint for a while.

She looked at the clock. He'd be counting the night's takings, preparing to leave.

She woke and he was standing above her. He put the car keys on the locker by the bed.

'Didn't mean to wake you,' he whispered. She opened her arms to him and he sank down onto the bed.

'I tried to stay awake. I got home an hour ago. I wanted to wait for you.'

'What for?' He buried his face in the soft warm flesh where her neck met her shoulder.

'Just did. We were hours at the hospital. Then we hung out until the sun came up.'

He undressed and got into bed behind her.

'Aren't you going to ask me how she is?'

'How is she?'

Silence. She heard him yawn.

'You woulda told me if she died. Let me guess. They stitched her up and put her to bed.'

It angered her that he was making light of it. And then her bad feeling dissolved at the touch of his warm body along the length of hers. She inhaled deeply. He kissed her between the shoulder blades. He gathered together all the locks and strands of her soft brown hair overflowing on the pillow and lifted them away from her neck, where he planted a chain of small kisses. He exhaled and she felt his breath on the back of her neck. His head went down heavily on the pillow.

'Zak?'

'Hm?'

'I told Angie she could stay here a while.'

'Cool.'

'You don't sound too happy.'

'No, it's cool. You did right to offer.'

Silence.

'But,' said Zak, 'she'll be back with Ray within a week.'

'I don't think so.'

He didn't reply.

'What makes you so sure?' Irritation crept into her voice despite herself.

'I know her. She loves him and hates him so she'll hang in there and get her revenge in a thousand little ways that no one else can see. She's got nothing else to do with her life and he has nothing else to do with his.'

She stiffened, uneasy to hear him say such things, and jealous at the suggestion that Zak knew Angie better than she did.

'Come on, babe. Don't be like that.' He said it gently. 'It's nothing got to do with you and me.'

He felt his head heavy, heavy on the pillow.

'Zak? You asleep?'

He was.

She woke shortly after 11 a.m., clearheaded and relaxed; the fog that had clogged her mind in the early hours had risen. She smiled and lingered when she saw that Zak had left a basket of strawberries at her breakfast place. During the week she rose early to have breakfast with him before she went to work and he went to bed, but at the weekends she'd sleep on and always find that he'd left something for her. Either a note or flowers picked by the roadside or something small he'd bought. She picked the reddest plumpest berry and bit.

Still with the rest of the strawberry between her fingers, she opened the screen door and stepped outside into the bright silent Sunday morning. She walked barefoot into the middle of the back lawn. The grass was turning yellow in patches. I should water it, she thought. She enjoyed the tickling of the grass on the tender soles of her feet as she looked up at the leaves at the top of the trees, shimmering in the light breeze. She finished the strawberry. The night before was far away and vague, like a dream or something that had happened a long time ago. But now the images of what had happened were coming back and began to trouble her, like a guilty secret she had tucked away. She recalled the cacophony of the band tuning up and Angie sprawled across the steps, the spectral lights of the strip.

She frowned. What was she doing eating strawberries in the sunshine? Why hadn't Angie called? It was late. What was going on?

She called the hospital and was put on hold. Then she was told that Angie had checked herself out at nine a.m. Laura paced across the living room. She went and looked in the spare room, aware even while she did it that she would not find Angie there. She grabbed the car keys and, though telling herself not to rush, drove too fast across town.

As soon as she turned into the street it was obvious which house was Ray's. He had two cars on his driveway stripped for repainting and one on blocks on the road. Ever since being laid off he spent his time tinkering with cars. It was an ordinary Sunday morning: children ran about shouting and playing and a couple sitting on their porch drinking coffee in the sunshine waved to Laura as she got out of her car. She rapped on Ray's door and waited. He took a long time answering. When he finally did appear he looked very different from the night before. He was dressed in a T-shirt and shorts. And he was barefoot, which made him appear smaller than usual. There was a white fleck of shaving foam where his dark curly hair met his cheekbone. His expression was almost one of bemusement. She stood for a moment looking at him, unable to say anything. Finally he blinked and said: 'I'm taking care of her now.'

And he closed the door.

Philip Ó Ceallaigh has lived in Romania since 2000. He received a Hennessy Award for poetry in 2001 and Arts Council bursaries in that year and 2004. He was short-listed for the Davy Byrnes Irish Writing Award in 2004 and his book of short fiction, *Notes from a Turkish Whorehouse*, will be published by Penguin Ireland in February 2006.

THE JUDGE

Paul Perry

Paul Perry was born in Dublin in 1972.
He studied at TCD and Brown University
and was a James Michener Fellow at the
University of Miami, where he won the
1997 UM Prize in Fiction. His work has
appeared in *Poet Lore*, *The Independent*, *The
Miami Herald* and other journals. (1998)

My father lies with his deep
sunken eyes closed. His fleshy
jowls and drooping lower lip sag in
mock disapproval. He looks to be
unimpressed with death, his chubby
fingers clasping each other as if he
himself were in prayer. Unimpressed
and a little impatient. The stiff black
suit he is wearing is an old one. He
wore it when I was a child. He wore
it when we went to Brittas Bay, where
he sat reading some book as we filled
his shoes with sand and buried his
feet as deep as we possibly could. The
suit is probably the kind of suit his
own father had been buried in. Stark

and rigid. Now look at the poor lovely man. Look at his powdered puckered face, his hands, the suit, his tie, a sombre navy necktie, a necktie he might have blustered over one early morning breakfast, tied and retied so that it sat perfect and still, the way he does now.

The room smells of dust and incense. The door is swinging open in the wind. The undertaker and his sons stand around awkwardly, you'd think they'd be used to this by now, coughing and squeaking in their eternally black shoes. What a sorry colour it is, black. Not even a colour. I yearn to place some small piece of brilliance on that face, whether it is a little rouge or a smear of lipstick. Yes, he looks a little obstreperous in death. Who knows where his soul is wavering, waiting, restless and alone, not unlike the way I might find him after he had fallen asleep in his study, his glasses teetering on the tip of his nose hinting at an unconscious incredulity at having left an article unfinished or an assignment incomplete.

My sister, Lena, arrives late. I have not seen her in four years. She is wearing orange lipstick. Her black skirt is too short and her eyes are narrower or closer together than I remember. What a surprise, she has brought a guest: her latest boyfriend, another fly-by-night. My mother, who has been twirling the gold cross my father gave her when they first met around her neck, welcomes her and they squeeze hands. Lena and my mother look strangely alike, which I also cannot recall noticing before. Lena smiles at me. There is lipstick on her teeth. My brother, Mark, has not looked up; he stands stiff in mournful attention. His eyes carry the dark stain of sleeplessness. Even when the undertakers close the casket, even then he does not look up, perhaps not wanting this forlorn image of our father to be his last. He has not looked at the judge, at his grey ashen face, and for a brief moment I feel like calling out to him. 'Stop it, Mark, and say good-bye to the old man. Don't be so stubborn. Forgive him.' But, I don't say anything and the casket closes.

My mother sounds like she is choking quietly, holding back her sobbing and keening with the decorum expected of one who has been the wife of an eminent judge. She weeps and shakes, her mouth open all the time as if she were about to say something, or as if she were actually saying something to the judge before he left her and had not finished what it was. We all cry, except for Mark who is standing still where he has been for the duration of this demented ritual of farewell, looking down at his shoes.

We called him the judge. At dinner time my mother would stand over a pot of steaming vegetables chiding us children to go to the study and get the judge, to interrupt and pull the judge away from his work, his deliberating. He was the judge, but he was also our daddy. He played with us, chased us and tasted our cooking. He told us stories and tucked us in, his hands smelling of cigar smoke, which to me was safe and reassuring.

Lena comments on how fitting the weather is. She says it's great to see me. The funeral is dreamlike. At one moment I am smiling at the quirky reminiscences of the judge's brother, Uncle B, on the parapet and the next the priest is throwing a handful of soil onto the dark box in which he lies. 'Ashes to ashes, dust to dust.' The priest disappears, vanishes like a messenger from another world, and the next thing I know the car horn is beeping. Lena sticks her head out the window and tells us we have to go. And we obey, me and mother shuffling towards the car in a light rain which is soothing because I am hot and perspiring. Mark is in the car too, sitting in the back seat, sighing, looking a little relieved actually.

There are people in the house when we return. How strange, the same faces, drinks in hand, forced smiles, reserved nods of the head, snickers and jokes, children running to the bathroom and watching television. The only thing missing from this gathering and past ones is the Christmas tree, the torn wrapping paper and presents and, of course, my father the judge. Uncle B comes up to me and shakes my hand. He mumbles something I cannot comprehend. What I hate most is the false earnestness of mourning. Cry if you want, but don't wince meekly and pretend you understand.

'Where did it all go wrong?' Lena says in the kitchen, pouring herself another vodka, and I have to leave the room, to weep again, to tear at my hair and hate her. Mark leads me back to the kitchen.

'Where is your Dieter?' he asks. Dieter is my husband. Dieter has a case, I tell him. Mark looks at me disapprovingly. But, the truth is I didn't really want him here. I prefer to be without him. I don't want his strong German shoulder to lean on, his calmness or pedantic Saxon reassurance. He is fond of Ireland, the vacations, the pubs and countryside, but he would never live here. Everything is so unorganised to him. Somebody has broken a bottle in the front room. It is cleaned up with too much apology. People are talking about my father, sharing small anecdotes. But, at the centre of the conversation there is a silence, an unspoken malaise.

Lena is laughing, and the house feels cold. 'Hasn't changed much,' Mark says. But, it has. The photographs on the wall of me as a little girl look strange and foreign. I haven't lived here since I was fifteen. My father had been a judge a long time. Mark was studying in college. Lena and I were still in school. It was all over the TV.

Bombs, rubble, hospitals and politicians. Four people were killed. My mother bit her lip; her sisters were living in England. I remember Mark shaking his head. 'Hope they catch the bastard,' Lena said, which the authorities did do, extraditing a man back to Ireland and putting him on trial.

My father tried the case. And that as my sister well knows is where it all went wrong. Our house, haunted as it seems now, a residential suburban semi-D, was placed under twenty-four-hour armed guard. It was floodlit like a football field with detectives standing on the street. People at school jeered us. Mark became unhappy; Lena was hysterical. Notes in our lockers, rotten socks and dead pigeons, phone-calls, sneers and boycotts: that was our lot.

My father had been a calm man, full of gentle humour; he walked the dog on Sunday, supped a pint in the local, went to a rugby match and kept to himself. When people met him, they nodded their heads in respect. But then we started receiving hate mail and death threats. I remember seeing my father's photograph in the newspaper, a dull black and white print as if he was the criminal. I went to school with his scowl on my mind and the smudged ink on my fingers. What had we done wrong? Why were we being made to leave our home and country for another one, where the food and people and customs were different, where we all felt dreadfully isolated, most of all my father, the judge.

The criminal appeared on TV, his family standing beside him. He was praised for not shooting more gardaí when he had the chance to. People turned against my father, though he had never hurt anyone. He became the quarry, the hunted pariah, so that police protection was not enough. We became the prisoners and didn't sleep at night. Hotel Insomnia, Mark used to call the house. 'Welcome,' he would sneer at breakfast. 'Will you be staying long?'

The living room window was smashed one night. Two Jewish friends of my parents sympathised. They had ex-perienced the same. But they stayed in Dublin while we moved to Hamburg, Germany. 'Don't worry,' my father said, 'I'm not selling the house. We'll come back to it yet.' I had always planned on coming back earlier, but then I met

Dieter and one thing led to another. I too practise law in Germany. Mark is a barrister in Dublin. Lena has her own problems with the law.

I remember one dark starless night, the new friends I had made suggested we go to the Reeperbahn. We were joking and laughing, sneaking in and out of the lewd clubs, spying on the dancers and the prostitutes, when I saw him, the judge, sitting in a seedy peep show slumped over a glass of flat beer doing the crossword puzzle, alone and pathetic. I don't know if he saw me, pushing my friends out, running away into the dark alien streets, sobbing like I am now.

'Will you stop crying?' Lena says to me pouring me another drink. 'Did he leave her anything?' she adds crudely. My mother who had walked into the kitchen hears her and replies dourly, 'Yes, Lena, he left me enough money, but not enough memories.'

The guests, if I can call them that, leave. My father might have been in his study and we might have been waiting for my mother to choose one of us to go and get him for his tea. Mark is still stiff with grief; his long fingers grip the end of his jacket and he gazes at the piano in the next room, the piano he practised on as a child for my father. He looks at it with grave misgiving as if the old broken thing that has not been played since we'd left for Germany is about to break into a tantalising ghost trio of its own accord.

'Make me a drink,' my mother says, directing the request at no one in particular. My hands are numb, but I lift them to the bottle and pour. She sits down at the kitchen table where the half-eaten sandwiches lie. 'It never felt like home again, did it?' she mumbles, or I imagine her to mumble, because the truth is I can't hear what she is saying. She coughs. The phone rings inappropriately in the gentle yellow and blue coloured kitchen. Lena lurches for it, and of course, it is for her. She talks too loud.

Mark's voice is hoarse. 'Does anyone else want a drink?'
The numb blanket of drink, ah, yes, cover us O Lord. I
remember telling Mark about the judge in the seedy club in
Hamburg. He looked at me then and sneered, 'Holding
court, was he?' A little later Mark returned to Dublin.

'So what's the plan?' Lena said putting down the phone.
'No plan,' my mother said, looking Lena in the eye. 'You
have my number if you need anything,' Lena says leaving by
the back door. Mark loosens his tie, sits down beside my
mother and holds her hand. 'I'll miss him,' my mother says,
'the grumpy old bastard.' She laughs. 'He became so bad
tempered in his old age, the poor man; everything annoyed
him. I think I did, too. I still loved him of course. Do you
think he knew that? Do you? It's funny, his own father had
fought in the Civil War.'

The phone rings again and I am reluctant to pick it up,
but I do. I have the surreal notion that it is my father. But, it
isn't. It is Dieter, my husband, calling from another world.
We talk in that curt, efficient way I have come to appreciate.
He tells me he loves me, sternly but assuredly, and I believe
him and it gives me strength. Germany was clean, well
ordered and humourless. I met Dieter at a newsstand. He was
in love with Ireland before he was in love with me. When I
put down the phone Mark is leaving. His wife has arrived, an
Australian woman who has made tea and brought a little
brightness into the dark and sombre house. As they leave I
want to ask them to take me and my mother with them, to
take us out of this cursed and forsaken bungalow. I would
have gladly looked back at its burning frame, revelled in its
destruction, but they leave, and we say a meek goodbye.

'What are we supposed to do?' my mother says. I
purposely misunderstand her and suggest cleaning up. She is
shuffling a pack of cards. I have no idea where they came
from and the exercise seems absurd to me. We clean up and

return to the kitchen, eating and drinking again, calming ourselves. I turn on the radio, and turn it off, irritated. Things should be still, without noise, without distraction, because for some reason, I still feel him here as if he has not gone yet, as if he is hanging on still saying goodbye.

We shuffle into the bedroom. My mother is looking for something. Her little hands search through the drawers. She pulls out handkerchiefs, musty and unused, pipes of all descriptions full of the dense odours of longing, a life of pondering, pensive walks and headaches. What is she looking for? His aftershaves, his ties, his shoes and underwear, what will she do with them? Donate them, perhaps, to some charity, burn them? She pulls out another deck of cards, reminding me of my father's penchant for gambling – his only vice, he would say – soiled by ink-smudged hands that had handled newspapers, journals, nineteenth-century novels and history books. I stand looking at her, my mother. She is older, ageing now even as I watch her.

Her head is in the closet where his shirts hang like lost children, small orphans, and there are his shoes, how sad they look, no longer to feel the heave and weight of his contemplative steps. She flicks through the jackets and shirts like the pages of a book and walks into the bathroom where a pair of his false teeth lie ignominiously disembodied. What will she do with all this? Throw it all away? What will she do with his subscriptions and prescriptions? What can she do, but cancel them.

She walks into the front room and opens the drinks cabinet. 'Another drink is it, mother?' I ask, but she does not hear me. The cabinet is full of his favourite liquors. Half-drunk bottles of scotch, ageing whiskeys and awaiting wines. What will she do with these intoxicants, poor woman? My mother. Would she scoff them down in one foul self-piteous night, pour them down the drain or let dust settle on their dark exteriors? What will she do without him?

In the front room, in a bookcase, she finds what she has been looking for: an old royal red photograph album. She sits on the floor and opens it up; a couple of photographs fall out. Sad black and white ones of the two of them as youngsters – they must have known each other all their lives – as newlyweds, my mother unable to hide her joy and pride, him in his robes, the kids, me, Mark and Lena. This treasure of the past does not disturb my mother the way I imagine it might. I crouch down beside her and together we arrange, fix and order the photographs into their neater places in the album. After a while without speaking, she closes the album abruptly and takes it to his armchair where she sits down.

I light some candles and sit in the sofa beside her. I try to sleep, but the ignoble picture of the family at the airport fleeing our home all those years ago comes back to me in fits and starts, the way we scurried away as if we had done something wrong. Why father could your almighty law, your scales of right and wrong, not save us? Where are you? Why aren't you here to put her to bed?

But it is I who gently wake her and as soon as I do I wish I hadn't. She looks at me with confusion and sadness. I have taken her away from some dream where she was with him; maybe she was dreaming about when they had first met in that pub in Baggot Street. I want to say sorry. I take her by the arm and lead her to her bedroom and put her under the covers. I sit on the edge of the bed like he had done before he went to bed so many times. I stroke her hair like he might have. I tell her it's all right. I tell her it's all right like you might have, daddy. But I want you here. I want you to come to me with your smoke stained hands. I want you to kiss my forehead and stroke my hair, to spin me a yarn and tuck me in farther, farther into the tight warm comfort of home as we once knew it; push me farther into that, daddy, father, judge, sir, papa, tell me you love me again, tell me what your verdict is on the day. Tell me who is guilty and who is innocent? Tell me, father, can any of us be saved?

Paul Perry won the Hennessy New Irish Writer of the Year Award in 1998. His first collection of poems, *The Drowning of the Saints*, was published in 2003 by Salmon. In 2002 he won the Listowel Prize for Poetry. Currently he is Writer in Residence for the University of Ulster.

BIG MOUTH

Blánaid McKinney

Blánaid McKinney was born in Enniskillen
in 1961 and read Politics at Queen's
University Belfast. When this story was
published she lived in London and was
Greenwich Area Manager with Greenwich
Waterfront Development Partnership. Her
work had been published in *Phoenix Irish
Short Stories.* (1998)

Aribatswa and Oubykh. As far as I
know, each has only one speaker
left, an old man and an old woman.
They could both be dead now, I suppose. Aribatswa is (or was) a New
Guinea language. Oubykh is (or was)
a language of the Caucasus. There are
ten thousand languages in the world.
There have been half a million since
we first started talking to each other.
In the next 100 years, half the
10,000 will die. Here in Australia,
over 300 languages have died in the
last 100 years. I know about these
things. I know about languages.

When I spotted what I thought was a familiar face in the mall three weeks ago, I wished I could've gotten close enough to hear him speak. But I didn't. I backed off and went home. It wasn't him anyway. It couldn't have been him.

I like Australia. It's a perky place. I've been here nine years and the energy of it still startles me. Ever since the Malaysians and Filipinos and Japanese moved in, it's become even more interesting. I still have plenty of money and I invested wisely. But I work anyway. When I'm not driving the cab, I read books. The kids don't bother me. She looks after them, keeps them out of my way, mostly. I still get angry when I remember those stupid taxi-drivers in New York, where I was holed up for a while. Those stupid, dumb fucks couldn't even speak English! How can they get you to where you want to go if they don't even speak the language? Fucking Mexicans. And Lithuanians. Jesus. There were three things that were the same the world over: the taxi-drivers, the big, balloon graffiti and the sound of couples fighting in the hotel room next door. I lost count of the number of hotels they put me up in. Well, I'm settled now. I've fitted in. And I keep my mouth shut.

It is said that the serpent that seduced Eve spoke Arabic, the most persuasive of all languages, that Adam and Eve spoke Persian, the most poetic of all languages, and that the Angel Gabriel spoke Turkish, the most menacing of all languages. Well, that's probably what started all the trouble; what we had there, as Cool Hand Luke might have observed, was a failure to communicate. Me, I speak English and I speak Latin. Sometimes I speak Latin at the dinner table to her and the kids, just to piss them off. She's okay; convict stock, with an addiction to prayer and girl-guide sensibilities. The kids, two boys, are eight and six, with lazy, soggy 'Strine accents that drive me crazy. Why can't they speak properly? My Belfast accent may not be the prettiest sound in the world, but I've worked on it, softened it, and I've kept my grammar as tight as a drum.

Getting involved, for me, was an easy, snobby, slovenly business. I didn't believe. Not like the others – the lads, the missionaries, the Boys. Oh, they believed alright; they believed so hard it made my teeth hurt, that bunch of pained guignols, with their Gaelic classes and their unimpeachable republicanism and their soothing folk pornography. Morons. But someone studying Linguistics and Latin at Queen's University was a trophy recruit and untrackable. It was just an academic poser for me. I just wanted to find out if I could do it, and being regarded as a respectable parasite didn't bother me at all.

Not only could I do it, I was good at it. Lookout mainly. Driver occasionally. I didn't see much but I always kept next day's newspapers. It was easy, fun even, and I didn't have to share their simian enthusiasm to get away with it. Each death was an end-of-the-pier punchline. I was an antiseptic ab-straction, an antidote to their cavalier, petulant cabaret. They knew I didn't believe but, for some reason, they trusted me anyway. They knew I could keep my mouth shut.

It was a pleasant two years; Latin during the day and the odd gig at night. There was no money in it, of course, but I enjoyed skimming with them, getting them to safety, listening to their vicious, beige tales afterwards. They were so proud of themselves. We divided our time between Lavery's and the Washington, drinking, plotting, holding industrious seminars in planned bloodshed. It was almost playful. I enjoyed Belfast back then, with its malicious accent and miraculous pubs. The pubs were the best thing about it. A Lorelei of towns. Pubs full of chesty rhetoric and a gallimaufry of weary menace and, occasionally, that brand of hatred so delicious I just knew it would cheer me up no end. Everyone played their part; I just didn't bury myself in the role. A friend, an actor who knew nothing of my life, got himself a job with the BBC, doing voice-overs for Gerry Adams. When he told me that, he couldn't understand why I had laughed so hard. Then the ban was lifted and he couldn't afford to feed himself. That thought made me laugh even harder. But despite having to listen to the boys' loud, flabby protestations of faith, and their Chaplinesque intentions towards some poor bastard or other, the pubs were fun. I didn't care; as long as I had my Latin and my pubs and my extra-curricular night time excitement, I was perfectly content.

Looking back, I think even their enthusiasm for language irritated me. The more windy and extravagant, the better they liked it. And Irish was just perfect. A language where 'to bury' and 'to plant' both employ the same verb. Perfect. A tongue of the air and the earth and the wind; so unlike English, which is the language of castles, of steel, of man-made structures and of perfect, intelligible expression. Good for making plain, for giving instructions. But Latin – now that was a different matter. No bandying about there. Clear expression of thought and even clearer integrity of purpose. Stern lapidary sentences, total functionality and a formal, divine polish which could express in one quarter of the space what any other tongue could say. While everyone else was brushing up on their *Brúidiúlacht*, and their *Díograis*, and their *Creideamh*, I was amusing myself by translating modern terms into Latin. I got as far as *Exterioris paginae puella* for 'cover girl', *Ictus a metro undecimo* for 'penalty kick' and *Longior taenia cinematographica* for 'movie'. They thought I was making fun of them. I was. And I didn't give a shit. But when we went on a job, they knew that, despite my indolent indifference, I would not fuck up. And I never did. What happened on the Ormeau Road was not my fault.

The cops just got lucky. After the boys came running into Bradbury Place, I gunned the motor up and took off down Botanic Avenue, into Rugby Road, Agincourt Avenue, through the Holy Land and up to seventy. Then that bastard in the Granada cut me off and we ended up crashing into the Ormeau Bridge. Well they just took off, leaving me with whiplash and a broken ankle. Two minutes later the RUC arrived and, well, that was me. After four days in hospital I was carted off to Castlereagh.

I told them nothing. For six days I remained completely silent. Not a word passed my lips and it drove them insane. They punched me, kicked me, slapped me, held a gun to my head, threatened to kill my parents, kept me awake for three days and then punched me some more and I didn't say one fucking word. They screamed and hollered until they trembled. They flailed around the room, making hysterical, seismic threats. They even tried the nice-cop/nasty-cop routine. I almost began to feel sorry for them. Nothing like silence to send a cop gradually, caustically bonkers. I didn't care. It wasn't loyalty that kept me quiet. And I am not brave. I'm just choosey about the people I talk to. After that, there was nothing for them to do but half-heartedly thump me some more. *Qui tacet consentire videtur.* Silence gives consent. But, bruises or no, I won. I wore them out. My body hurt for a long while afterwards but I won because they had nothing on me, and on the seventh day I was bailed.

As far as I remember, that's when things changed. Now, I am not a petulant man, nor a man who would expect to be lionised for his stoicism. But some things deserve an appropriate measure of recognition. Otherwise nothing makes any sense, and the things that we do and say are meaningless. I did not expect praise from my runaway comrades – they were too acutely aware that my participation was more academic than heartfelt – but even so, I wasn't prepared for the wall of silence when we got together in the pub two days after my release. No mention was made. They avoided my eyes. They shifted uneasily in their seats, downed their pints too quickly and discussed future projects with a studied, childish earnestness that suddenly made me annoyed. All that gallant jabber. It was as if I wasn't there. They knew I hadn't talked, but it was as if the significance of what I had done had been consigned to some embarrassing kill-file. It wasn't what I had done that shamed them. It was the fact that it was me who had done it. Me, the one who didn't care and didn't believe. At that moment, I made a decision. Oh — don't get me wrong, it wasn't petulance; loyalty was not the reason I protected them. And resentment was not the reason I betrayed them. It is simply that it was so easy. And communication is so important. I decided I wanted to be listened to. That would make a nice change.

The following morning I presented myself at the nearest police station, discreetly of course, and after various phone calls and incredulous panics and breathed, ignored obscenities, I was taken to see the very men who had kicked the shit out of me the previous week. They were very jumpy, and amazed by my benign calm, my utter lack of belligerence, and even more amazed by my proposal.

For a fortnight I sang like a bird. I told them everything. I talked so much they couldn't keep up. It was thoroughly enjoyable. The money would be useful, of course, and I always wanted to travel, but it was the nattering I liked best. I gave them names, addresses, physical descriptions, times, places, sights, sounds, smells, idiosyncrasies, all in a deadpan blah that I knew impressed the hell out of them. I was a shiny one-man documentary, a walking karaoke, with lyrics and sleeve notes to spare, a destroyer of silence. They bristled with excitement as I drawled on, changing their cassette tapes and sharpening their pencils and sucking on their biros, not knowing that I couldn't have cared less whether they used the information or not. I kept thinking about Dionysius, Tyrant of Syracuse, who incarcerated

suspects in a fifty-foot high prison, carved in channels into
the rock in such a way as to resemble the human ear. Even
the slightest whisper by the prisoner would waft its way
upwards and, eventually, be used against him. The Ear of
Dionysius. Excellent idea. Mind you, I made it a lot easier
for them than that. £175,000 and a new identity – I think
that's fair.

I saw him again. Two weeks ago, in the mall. And there
was another man with him, with the kind of rounded
shoulders I hate and remember. It's pretty funny actually, the
way memories sneak up on you; ten years on and I still see
their faces, hear their adenoidal, Andytown rasps and
Belfast's moody, playpen racket, a town oscillating between
noisy cod-fundamentalism and baggy, raving silliness.
Sometimes I miss it. The day before I left for good, in 1980,
I was looking out of the window of my hotel room on a
grey, miserable November afternoon. And travelling slowly
down the middle of Great Victoria Street was a huge
transporter vehicle, carrying eight gleaming, sparkling silver
DeLoreans from the plant. Cutting through the granite and
the gloom, it was the most beautiful thing I'd ever seen. We
used to see that a lot. I never quite got over it. And then,
with the cocaine and whatnot, the plant went belly-up, and
that was that. I still miss the place. That's why I still see faces
I think I recognise, and rounded shoulders and pigeon toes
that just give me the creeps.

I go to the mall a lot during the day. I like it. Well,
actually I hate it, but I can't stay away. Nothing cheers me
up more than an afternoon spent marvelling at the orch-
estral stupidity of people, their gorgeous consumers' body
language, the picking up and the putting down, the poking
and prodding, the disdainful pretence that they're not really
shopping, oh no – they're just perusing, like beatific art
collectors. Christ, they make me sick. And the teenagers are

the worst, with their faux-funky lolling around, their vacuous vocab and their sunny hairdos. I blame television. No – I really do. I don't let my kids watch TV. I got rid of it three years ago. They probably hated me for that. I don't care. TV has no shame, and these kids have no stories. They have answers to questions they never even asked and they think it makes them grown up. They have adjusted to incoherence. TV allows no secrets and secrets are important. My kids didn't understand that and I was sick of their crying and whingeing so I carried the damn set into the garden and took a sledgehammer to it. I didn't get any arguments after that.

You can tell a lot about someone from their clothes too, and the mall is a good place to watch for that. Especially the women, with their bewildering squall of colours and styles. There are two women who meet outside the bookshop every lunchtime. They're deaf. When they speak it's too fast to try to follow; their hands flutter about like pallid peacocks. Their fingers nibble and scrawl on the air so quickly it almost makes me dizzy. I like watching them. There's another guy who sits for hours eating rolls and drinking Coke and, I swear, one of these days I'm going to have to stop myself from punching him. He's disgusting. He must weigh at least 250 lbs. He's enormous, and he just sits there with his hideous rolls of fat and his too-tight T-shirt and his messy, pudgy fingers. I hate him. Because I can't read him. How can you read a body language that's buried, paralysed, imprisoned under all that? And I hate the assistant in the newsagent. He must've been in a fire or something. You can't tell *shit* from that shiny, immobile mask of a face. People like that, they don't play fair.

Something odd happened last week. A parcel arrived in the post. It smelled funny and the paper was greasy. I opened it. It contained a calf's tongue, fresh and quite bloody. She wouldn't stop asking me about it. How was I supposed to know what it meant? It was probably a mistake, or maybe our butcher's gone funny in the head. I gave it to the dog and told her to just shut up and stop going on about it. I didn't tell her about the note.

That night, I had a weird dream. I dreamt that I could speak every language on the planet, except English. I was impressive and redundant at the same time. It felt great. But I woke up feeling uneasy and I didn't know why. Ten years is too long a time. I'm on the other side of the world. It just wouldn't make any sense.

We sat around the dinner table last night. The three of them said grace, with hands clasped and eyes screwed shut, their faces a picture of mournful fervour. I held my breath, as usual, and just let them get on with it. Then the six-year-old announced that a man had approached him on the playground with a message for his father.

I froze in mid-swallow.

'What was the message?'

'Payback.'

The kid began to laugh as if he found the word funny, but he stopped laughing when I grabbed him by the neck and screamed at him to tell me what the man looked like, what kind of accent he had. Then he started to cry and stammer and he couldn't talk, and she was belting me across the shoulders and squawking at me to put him down. What was wrong with me? she demanded, tears streaming down her face. Had I gone mad? I didn't tell her anything. I just walked out. I've never told her anything. She hasn't a clue. My past is an encyclopaedia of banished unwhisperables because that's the way I wanted it to be. So I walked out and after a while I couldn't hear the sonic whine of her weeping anymore.

I have never understood passion, or even bumbling enthusiasm. What's the point? It simply broadcasts damage and wounds effortlessly wherever it goes. Their belief meant a bullet in the head. Her rapturous domesticity meant tears when she had to tell the kids Santa didn't exist. I wasn't on some kind of intestinal campaign. I just didn't care. In Japanese, the characters for 'busy' translate as 'mind dying'. I had no truck with their scruffy, unstable cannibalism; I had a new life and a cool new baptism. Okay, maybe they had a point about their lost land and their lost tongue and the enforced translations that produced the ugliest aural geography in the world. But I knew that underneath their casual brutalism and forlorn whining was a big fucking gap, a huge hole, a hectoring emptiness that screamed the truth at them – that if they didn't have the Cause, they wouldn't exist. And they tried to convince themselves that the world is simply fascinated by what goes on there. Well, the world doesn't give a shit. The world's got more important things to think about. The world doesn't give a rat's arse and every time they looked at me they knew it was true. Cretins.

It's morning. I'm in the kitchen with the six-year-old. I'm chopping carrots. The back door opens and he's standing there. He is holding a gun. He looks a little older. He's wearing a suit. He looks good. I don't know what to say. So I say, 'Why?'

He smiles at me.

And points the gun at my son's head.

'*Le díoltas.*' I don't understand. It's Irish. I don't understand the word. Then he says '*Ultio.*'

Latin for 'revenge'.

'*Maniae infinitae sunt species.*'

Fools are numberless. He's made an effort. Is it a tribute or is it scorn? I can't tell. He begins to talk and his gun hand never wavers. The child lets out a tiny chirrup of fear, then is silent and motionless. The man talks and his voice, older now, has a beauty that is venomous and pure, a timbre I have never forgotten. It is intolerably clear. He speaks of loyalty and I am hypnotised by the unimaginable depth of his conviction. He really means it. His smile is solicitous, almost kind, as if he feels sorry for me. Sorry for my lack of faith, for my poor, empty heart that has never belonged anywhere. He talks of courage. He tells me that I am dumb. That I have always been dumb.

And then he pulls the trigger and my son's blood is everywhere.

When he was small and babbling, his elder brother would translate for him.

His name was John.

I can't think of anything to say, so I don't bother saying anything. I keep thinking about how good he looks in that suit. The old man and the old woman. Eighty-three consonants and three vowels. And no one left to talk to. This strikes me as funny. I don't know why, but I start to laugh. I laugh uncontrollably, because I can't think of any words to say. He is still softly speaking as he glides out the door but I am not listening. I am alone and walking in blood, swaying and speechless.

Since this story was published Blánaid McKinney has published two widely acclaimed books: a short story collection, *Big Mouth* (London, Phoenix House, 2000); and a novel, *The Ledge* (Phoenix House, 2002).

2000

THE SEPARATION

Paul Grimes

Paul Grimes was born in England but now lives in Kilnaboy, Co. Clare, where he teaches natural health techniques. He has always written but never thought of submitting any of his stories for publication until he joined a writing group conducted by David Rice. (2000)

The two men had been walking together in silence for the past fifteen minutes when they reached the top of the hill. They stopped by unspoken agreement and began to consider the view. Now that they had reached the top of the hill the mountain range that they had been partially seeing for some time had come completely into view. And it was this sight that was consuming their attention. The older man, though he had seen the sight many times, was lost in deep concentration. The younger man had never seen the sight before and his eyes and mind moved quickly among the mountains.

After a few minutes the younger man broke the silence.

'Do you think Mum was an addict too?'

The older man seemed irritated, almost distressed by the question. He took a long while to think about what his brother had said.

'I'm just thinking,' the younger man continued. 'What with me being addictive, my drinking and the other stuff. And you admit yourself to being a workaholic. Maybe Mum was an addict and that's where we get it from.'

'I think you need to forget about Mum. You can't dwell on her. You've got to get past her, Terry. You've got to get on with your own life,' the older man said.

'I know,' said Terry. 'I know you're right, Brian. But it's hard to get past that. When I was in the unit and I had the counselling I could never quite figure where the addictive stuff had come from. Whether it was in my blood or it was something that had happened. I think it would help me to know.'

'What did the doctors say?'

'They didn't tell me. They don't tell you things. They listen to what you are saying. I think they want you to tell them. It has to come out of your own mind.'

Brian said nothing; he was imagining having to bring his own thoughts and feelings up from the places where they were kept. He watched Terry bent over talking to the dog.

'He's a good dog, Bri.'

'He's old now,' Brian replied.

They both watched the dog, a scruffy black and white sheepdog.

'Do you want to go back now?' Brian asked.

'I don't mind.'

'Molly will have the dinner on.'

'OK then. I'm hungry.'

They turned away from the mountains and began to walk back down the hill. To anybody who did not know, they did not look like brothers. There was an age difference of about five years but they seemed to be separated by so much more than that. Brian was a large, stocky man. He was almost bald except for the brushed back tufts of gingery hair above his ears. His moustache was ginger too but flecked with grey. He looked out onto the world through pale brown eyes that watched from behind steel-rimmed glasses. He was clothed in an old tweed sports jacket and corduroy trousers.

Terry came from a different generation than Brian. He had a full head of dark brown curly hair. His face was thinner and more attractive. Terry's clothing was younger: a sports sweatshirt, jeans, and trainers. He could have almost been Brian's son. Except that there was something very old about his blue eyes; they were busier and more alert than those of his brother.

Brian had always suspected that they had different fathers. There was so much about them that was different. He had never shared this suspicion with Terry. Terry's difficulties with the memory of their mother were complicated enough.

'I didn't know mum as much as you think I did,' Brian said.

'You were older though,' said Terry.

'I was just seven when she left us — I was a little boy.'

Terry said nothing.

'I only remember a few things. I spent more time living with Gran than I did with Mum,' said Brian.

'Why couldn't we have lived with Gran?'

'I don't know. I don't think she had the room. Or she was too old. I think she wanted us to go in the home because she thought it would be better for us. She didn't have a lot of money either. She thought we would be better looked after in the home.'

'That was a fucking joke,' said Terry.

'I know, but she did the best she could.'

'What was Mum like, Bri?'

'Jesus, Terry, I must have told you a thousand times. That was all you used to ask me in the home.'

'I know, but I forget. I was a kid then. We're older now. I want to hear you tell me again. I've been thinking a lot about Mum.'

Brian said nothing for a minute. The dog had brought him a stick and he was trying to get the dog to give it up.

'Put it down, Rex. Put it down.' The dog backed away; its tail was wagging furiously. It wanted to play but it did not want to give up the stick: that was also a game.

'Mum was very pretty,' Brian said. 'She was tall and slim and full of fun. She used to call me Boo Boo. That was after the cartoon. She was Yogi Bear and I was Boo Boo. Only she wasn't like Yogi Bear at all. She was full of light. She was quick and always on the go. When we were together it was always playtime. She wasn't like a mother, more like a crazy older sister. It was so good when she was happy and we were together – it made up for all the other times. And then the telephone would ring. She called the telephone her lifeline. She said it connected her to the world. As though the world was another place than where we were.

'The telephone would ring and she would be gone. Or a man would come to the flat. Or one of her girlfriends. And she would be gone. I would end up at Gran's and I might not see her again for days. Or weeks. That's all there is to say, Terry. There is no more.'

'I know,' said Terry.

They walked on again in silence. The dog was a hundred yards ahead of them now. Walking intently homewards, the stick in its mouth.

'Do you have somebody now?'

'Do you mean a girl?'

'Or a man,' Brian said softly.

'That upset you, didn't it?'

'I was upset about what had happened to you in the home. I knew it was those bastards that had messed you up.'

'Perhaps. I don't know. Maybe I was meant to be the way I am. Maybe it was even, you know, coming from a broken home. I mean, you were messed up too.'

'It was different for me,' Brian said.

'Your marriage broke up. You lost the kids. Your business went bust. Wasn't all that to do with where you came from?'

'I lost sight of things. I was working too hard. I was trying to build up the business. I took Anne for granted. That's about the worst thing you can do to a woman. She couldn't take it, me never being home. I don't think I'm very good at relationships. I try really hard but I just don't seem to know what to do. It's like some people are good at gardening and others can't even grow a weed. I'm no good at relationships.'

'What about Molly, then?' Terry asked.

'Things are better. I've learned a lot. I try really hard all the time.'

'I think we're the same like that,' Terry said. 'I can't manage relationships. I want too much from people. I suck them dry of emotion. I keep testing them all the time.'

'You don't believe people can love you,' Brian said.

'No. Well, I haven't had a lot of experience. You know, with Mum and all that.'

'And the home?'

'The home didn't help.'

'I thought you were tougher,' Brian said. 'You always seemed tougher when we were kids. You were tougher than me.'

'I think I was being tough for both of us. It all seemed to get to you more. I didn't know enough then. That was all I knew of the world.'

'But you weren't so tough?'

'When you went and I was on my own it was harder. They seemed to pick on me more after you went. Like they were paying me back for you escaping.'

'The beatings?'

'And the other stuff,' Terry said and looked away from the road.

'I'm sorry, Terry.'

'It wasn't your fault. It was harder afterwards. After I left the home. While I was there it was normal, the beatings and the abuse. Afterwards when I got out and tried to make my own way it was different. It was harder then.'

'I'm sorry,' Brian said again.

'They fucked me up, Bri. They fucked me completely up.'

'I shouldn't have left you there.'

'I don't blame you anymore for that, Bri. You had to get out.'

'I couldn't take you with me.'

'I know.'

'I was too young. I was only 16. I was only a kid myself. I got out as soon as I could.'

'I know, Brian. I'm not blaming you.'

'I was going to come back for you, I really was. But I got a job and then I had to find a place. I was trying to find somewhere good enough to bring you to. It just never happened. And then I met Anne. She loved me so much then, at first. I had to make a go of it.'

Terry said nothing.

'I used to think of you all the time. I knew what was happening to you in that place. I should have gone back to visit you. But I couldn't even do that.'

'That was hard for me, Bri. I kept thinking that one day you would turn up.'

'I'm so sorry.'

'I know, Brian. It's OK. I'm over that now.'

'I thought that's why you had come up here to see me.'

'What, come to blame you, you mean?'

Brian nodded.

'I don't blame you, Brian. Those were just the things that happened to us. We couldn't help it. We both tried to do the best we could.'

'Why did you come?'

'I came to see you.'

'Honestly?'

'Honestly, Bri. I came up to see you. I wanted to see you. I think something's changed in my life. And I wanted to get over what happened. You are all I have in the world.'

'I'm sorry, Terry. I really am.'

'It's over, Brian. It's gone past.'

Brian said nothing. He was conscious that Terry was full to the brim, that the tears were only a word away. They walked on in silence. The dog had stopped at the entrance to the house; it was waiting for them. It had dropped the stick into a pile of fallen leaves and its breath was soft on the autumn air.

Paul Grimes died at the age of fifty-two in October 2004. Paul had been writing all of his life but became more serious during his years living in Ireland. He was short-listed for the RTÉ Francis MacManus short story competition and he won the Bryan McMahon Short Story Prize. Paul was published in the *Sunday Tribune, The World of Hibernia, The Dubliner* and *Phoenix Irish Short Stories*.

LICK OF THE
LIZARD

Geraldine Mills

Geraldine Mills recently returned to her native Galway, having lived in Dublin for twenty years. Her short stories have won the Oki Award, the Moore Medallion, the North Tipperary Short Story Competition and the South Tipperary Short Story Competition, and they have been short-listed for the Fish Prize and the Francis MacManus Awards. A full-time mother to her two children, aged eleven and seventeen, she writes whenever she can steal some time away from housework, gardening and driving. (2000)

I am sweeping myself into the dust-bin. Every day I take the brush and run it along the wooden floorboards honeyed by age, marked and pitted by pots dropped in moments of un-coordination. I inch it into corners, sidle it around the legs of furniture so that when I arrive at the door, my brush has rounded up another day's gathering of myself. Little piles of dirty grey dust that cling to the sides of the plastic white bin liner. And what is it? Sloughed off skin cells. My skin cells. I cannot tell when I sweep up the bits whether it's an arm cell or a nail cell or a brain cell for that matter. I seem to gather into corners, in little puffballs that stick to the bristles of the brush that I have to comb off at the end of my sweeping like a weaver carding wool. I am already half-way towards burial.

I look at Lisa's fifteen-year-old skin, the softest, blemish free, the living bloom of youth upon her cheeks; the gloss of her black hair as it nests in around her ears, the bright-ness of her eyes. She walks around unaware of her beauty. That's what I don't like about her; she's too beautiful to be my daughter. She doesn't have to worry about sweeping her cells into the dustbin. Her cells are too busy still replicating and bouncing around with life force to be anxious about epidermis or collagen.

They say our cells are renewing themselves every day; that over seven years we have renewed our whole body so that we're really not the same persons we were seven years before. No wonder I have a problem with Lisa. She's not the person she was two years ago. All her cells have been changed and I am no longer dealing with someone I can make head or tail of. Someone I can like. She was a nice little girl once. Not any more; she blames me.

When I've finished sweeping I go and make myself a cup of tea. Lisa joins me when she comes in from school; leaves her bag quietly in the corner, hangs up her coat. She's not supposed to do that. She's supposed to fling her bag where I'll fall over it, throw her coat on the chair that will eventually slither onto the floor and get walked on so that I can scream at her and tell her I am sick of the way she treats her clothes. But no. She treads gently, angel-like, her brown eyes as clear as spring water, asks me would I like a biscuit.

She tells me a little about her day before she goes upstairs to do her homework.

We have been three years like this now. Ever since her father died, without a warning, leaving the two of us together without him to keep us apart. Lisa came back from basketball training one evening and found him in the kitchen slumped over the table as if he were asleep, his tea untouched, egg yolk stuck to his hair. When I returned from my night out with the girls I found her note on the table. She was in the hospital with him. I was too late. A stroke they said. Lisa cried for days. He was an old man when I married him but not old enough to die, I would have thought. And I swear he was her father though there's manys the biddy who would have liked to claim otherwise. She had neither his looks nor any of his ways so that Molly Heffernan claimed the fairies must have come and switched her when we weren't looking because we didn't put the tongs across the cradle. Maybe Molly's right, a little bit too smart for us all. Would mind mice at the crossroads. She doesn't say it but she walks with an air of one who keeps too much too close to her chest. I don't like that in a person. My daughter especially.

It was a while before I started to go out again. I wasn't going to be the fodder for their gossiping sodalities, or the theme for Father Toughy's Sunday sermon. A few of the smart buckos started sniffing around thinking I was easy prey now, God help their sense. Wives turned away from me at socials, put their hands possessively on their husbands' arms if I said more than hello to them. How were they to know that I wouldn't be bothered going for bacon and cabbage when I could now taste gourmet? That is why I was so pleased to see Dave.

He hadn't changed at all. At first when I saw him in the kitchen I thought it was just someone who reminded me of him. The way he was standing there with that careless look hanging around him. I wouldn't have seen him in all this time but then he took a drag on a cigarette and I was certain. I recognised the smell — a London, Kilburn High Road smell — and laughed to myself when Sal Fine sniffed the air and asked who was burning tealeaves on top of the range. His brain cells must be burning up quicker than mine, I thought, though how he kept his body cells together I couldn't understand, for his hadn't aged at all. Not like mine. Still the long legs, the lean flat stomach — a rarity in men of his age — his hair still long, the beginnings of grey.

I watched the old familiar way he combed his fingers through it and I was going back to that first smell of freedom as the boat sailed out of Dun Laoghaire and headed towards Holyhead. My first summer in London. The clunk of the train as it made its way across the night to arrive in Euston all baggy eyes from a rough crossing and lack of sleep. Here was a new world of cockney accents, porters with black faces, the smell of dirt smoke. I met up with the crowd from college that were over there before me. We got work in a hotel near James Park. One evening on my way home from a long shift skivvying, I was heading up out of the tube station. This lean body came hurrying down the steps and crashed into me and I would have tumbled back into the black hole of tunnel if he hadn't rushed out his hand and grabbed me. He insisted on bringing me back to his flat with the awful smell of gas on the air, sitting me down and running next door for two Turkish coffees that would support a spoon standing they were so black and thick. Then he took out his Rizla papers and rolled himself a smoke. It was the first time I smelled dope as he called it, the smell that was now all over Malachy Russell's kitchen.

I seldom saw my own flat after that, returning just to be there for the phone call that came as regular as the Angelus from Ireland every Friday evening. *Easy Rider* posters on the wall, 'Midnight at the Oasis' playing, the hard mattress on the floor. Every morning I headed off to work in the Park Hotel, my eyes dark from lack of sleep, where I bundled stained sheets into a trolley and replaced them with crisp clean ones. I renewed thin bars of soap, straightened bibles on lockers and returned in the evening to the warmth of his arms. How could I forget the evening I was cooking some dinner for the two of us when I burned my hand on the edge of the saucepan? I cried out with the pain and he just took my hand and put it to his mouth, licking it all over with his tongue. He told me he had a cure for burns from the time he was eleven. There he was sitting on a rock blistering from the sun when a lizard taking advantage of the heat darted across and licked him. I believed him, falling more and more in love with his strong thighs, his blond curly hair and his blue eyes. Foolishly believing he had such a cure until he slithered off and left me smouldering away without him.

So. He's here again. He had mentioned once to me about being a distant relation of Malachy's family but I had forgotten all about it until now. He doesn't recognise me at first but as the recognition dawns I can see his mind going over the last time we were together and a smile breaks out on his lips. We talk a little and then he asks if we can go somewhere quiet. We go out the door with his arm around my shoulder and Sal Fine's mouth as wide as the Shannon when she sees us go.

We go to a small pub in the next village. Not that it gives us much privacy. The news will be back in Malachy's kitchen before I have finished my first glass. I drink too much red wine and fall against his shoulder when we walk towards the car, laughing as I make various attempts to get into it and have to be helped. He plays John Lennon all the way home. He's still in never-never land.

I ask him in for some coffee when we get back. Lisa's still up. She's crouched over the kitchen table working on some project that has to be finished for her exam. She lifts her head.

'Hi,' she says quietly.

'Lisa, this is Dave, an old friend from the past I met at Malachy's wake. We're just having some coffee.'

'Well, I'll leave you so.' And with that she starts to fold up her books.

'What have you there?' Dave asks. 'It looks pretty complicated.'

'Not really. It's just a database for an accounting firm that has to be included in this project.'

As she goes into the details of the project I can see it happening before my eyes. Her devious little ways, her quiet voice that makes him incline his head even further to hear her explanations. When she looks up into his eyes I can see. He is being drawn in. Then she yawns, draws back her chair and says goodnight to us.

'She's gorgeous, isn't she?' he says when she has gone. 'But I'm not surprised. She'll have them crawling out of the woodwork before very long.'

'Not so sure about that. I know most mothers are supposed to think their daughters are beautiful but Lisa, she's a bit too quiet in her looks for my liking. There isn't a bit of me in her, or her father for that matter.'

'Her skin's like yours was,' he says touching my cheek.

'Was being the operative word.'

I feel the old green-eyed monster raising its head.

'No, you still look terrific. Are you doing anything tomorrow? Maybe we could meet in town for lunch.'

'I'd love that.'

Later as I cover my face with night cream, I remember the times when I couldn't sleep for want of him and how, when it was finally over, how I walked through St James Park with the trees about to turn knowing there would never be anyone like him.

We have a great lunch. He says he's thinking of staying around for a couple of weeks. The job in London isn't that important. It can wait. It was so long since he was home. It would be nice to be able to catch up on some old times. His questions about Malachy's death are full of concern. How hard it was for me bringing up a daughter alone. He wants to know all about her. This talk soon tires me. I say it is time to go home.

We return just as Lisa is coming back from school in her maroon gym slip and grey blouse.

Dave takes her bag from her and walks up the path with her, asking her about her day, the different teachers, things like that. She comes up to his shoulder, he leans down to her; she laughs. When we get in I pour us a drink. Dave slips into the chair by the window, crosses his legs. Lisa goes into the kitchen and starts to fry up some lunch for herself. Suddenly there's a scream from her. Dave runs into the kitchen before I even get to the door. Grease from the pan has jumped out and splashed her. And then I hear Dave saying, 'Don't worry, I have a cure for that.' And I know exactly what he's going to say. I can repeat it almost word for word. How he was once a small boy that sat on a rock and a lizard licked him and gave him a cure for burns. He is saying all of this while he is looking into her soft eyes and licking her hand. She is feeling the power of him as the smoke from the pan rises up into the ceiling and the fire alarm goes off. Neither of them does anything, so I run out into the hall swatting it with the dishtowel until I can disperse the smoke. The bleeping stops.

I take up the brush and start to sweep. Now I have my cells and Lisa's all mixed up together. Dave's cells don't fall off like ours, not in little pockets to be swept into the dustpan. When he grows out of his skin it gets tighter and tighter until it splits and it sloughs off in one go. Just like the lizard that licked him.

A regular contributor to RTÉ radio, Geraldine Mills's first collection of short stories was published by Arlen House in 2005. She has published two collections of poetry, *Unearthing Your Own* and *Toil the Dark Harvest*, with Bradshaw Books, Cork. Her monologue 'This Is from the Woman Who Does' was premiered at the Provincetown Theatre, Mass., USA in October 2004.

EYES LIKE
MARTY FELDMAN

Kieran Byrne

Kieran Byrne lives in Ballyfermot and has
worked as a freelance journalist. He has
had some stories published in small
magazines. He is a member of the Inkwell
Writers' Group. (2000)

Motherajaysus – we're on the
bleedin' telly!'

The Sony portable was skating
backwards across the table as Froggie
stabbed at its screen with a nicotine
finger. 'It's us! Look, there's you ... and
here's me, over here. It's us, man! Us!'

It was us, all right. Me and Froggie
Brennan, right there on the gogglebox.
Snared by the Underground security
camera as we ransacked the vending
machines.

'Jesus. We've made the news,' I muttered.

'Fame at last, what?' roared Froggie.

On screen was a Barbie doll re-
porter standing on the platform of a

dark tube station. The station could have been anywhere; they all looked the same and we'd already done hundreds. Then the picture switched back to the black and white footage, the shot of me and Froggie doing the machines, except this time the camera lens panned a little to the left, zoomed in ...

Froggie roared. 'Fuck me! It's you!'

Me, face pale and grainy as a 1940s photo, fag dangling from mouth as my plundering hands went to work on the soft-drinks machine.

Then the camera lens abandoned me and turreted to the right where Froggie, with his shirt-tail hanging out, had just finished cleaning out the fag machine. The camera lingered on him, as if sensing that more was to come.

And that's when Froggie did it.

He looked up.

'Jesus! Froggie! Why'd yeh look up?!'

'I didn't!'

'Yeh did!'

Just five seconds, but long enough, plenty of time to create astonishment on viewers' faces.

Because in those five seconds, they would've seen Froggie's eyes.

Thousands of astonished Londoners, staring at their television sets. I sensed them from St John's Wood to Brixton, from Shepherd's Bush to Whitechapel; their dinner forks halting on the way to their mouths, their beer glasses frozen in mid-air, their knitting needles dropping a stitch. Squealing kids calling their mothers to come in and take a look at the man on the telly with the big, big eyes.

Froggie's had the disease since he popped out of his mother in the Coombe. He makes much of the fact that he was born the day they blew Nelson out of O'Connell Street. I can't say whether he's heard the jokes about it, the jokes that claim it was blast damage that puffed up Froggie's eyes to the size of rugby balls. Well, maybe not that big. But certainly as big as golf balls, which is why they call him Froggie. Funny thing, that – Froggie doesn't mind the nickname, but fellas who mention the eyes usually end up in the Mater. Maybe that's why people won't slag him to his face: Froggie's very good at cracking skulls. He's also a dab hand with a Stanley knife.

Now he was a telly curio, those huge whites of eyes gazing at the camera lens.

'Jesus, Froggie,' I muttered. 'Why didn't you wear your shades?'

'Wouldn't worry too much about it,' he smiled. 'Only about five million people watchin'.'

I tried to smile. 'Froggie, yeh were only short of pullin' a mooner for the camera.'

His huge eyes swivelled in on me. Sometimes when he looks at me like that his eyes seem huge but lifeless. Eyes of a great white shark.

'Are you tellin' me that anybody'd know it was me on that camera?' he asked seriously. 'Is that what you're tellin' me? Camera picked your face up as well.'

'Froggie, don't take the piss.'

He nodded. The eyes seemed to deflate a little, like they'd been stricken with a slow puncture. He smiled mischievously. 'Yeah. I suppose. Yeh'd hardly miss me, would yeh?' He reached over and took one of my cigarettes. 'That's it then, Sundance; looks like it's back to the sites.'

'Not for me. I'm headin' back to Dublin.'

Froggie looked thoughtful as he circled the room, smoking furiously. 'Come on, man. We're just creamin' off a bit of small change.'

'Small change,' I echoed. 'Yeah. That's why we're on the bleedin' news.'

'Relax, Sundance.' He seized the Thunderbird bottle and

hoisted it high. 'A toast! To black collar crime and the scammers of the world. Next stop, the *Cook Report*.'

'They'll bang us up in the Scrubs,' I said.

Froggie grinned. 'So we made the news. Big deal. CID'll be too busy chasin' Irish fellas with Semtex stashed down their jocks.'

Still, it didn't look good.

We knew about the security cameras, but we also assumed the coppers would see us as small-time. I mean, the idea wasn't that sophisticated. All we did was take sheets of lead from the building site, cut them up into little circles and cover tenpenny pieces with them, which we pushed in coin slots. The machines work on weight sensor, and they're fooled by thinking the 10ps are actually 50ps. All we did then was push the 'cancel' button, as if we've changed our minds about buying, and out drops a 50. Half an hour later the machine's full of lead and your pocket's full of dosh.

Kept us in fags and booze and probably would've saw us through to our twenty-second birthdays, if only we'd stayed wide and played it cute. It also freed us from the building site in Westminster, where we'd grafted like muck birds in the shadow of Big Ben.

'Still meetin' yer woman?' Froggie asked me. 'Y'know, your one in Piccadilly. All tits an' arse.'

'You mean Tracie?'

'Was that her name?' A smirk touched his lips. His eyes swelled a little. Sometimes I imagine a tiny operator working a foot pump behind those eyeballs.

'Prick-teasin' smile, micro-skirt. Got a glimpse of suspender, too. Always been a jammy bastard with the women, haven't yeh?'

I shifted uncomfortably on the sofa. 'World's fulla women, Froggie. You go for one an' yeh miss, just keep shootin' till yeh hit the bull's-eye.'

'Didn't like my bull's-eyes though, did she?' he said

quietly. His fingers toyed with the Stanley knife, the one we'd been using to cut up the sheets of lead. 'Birds like that really piss me off. Think their fannies're made of gold.'

I let out a sigh. I knew he'd harp on all night about it, about how I swiped away his chance of a bit of skirt. This was the fourth time today he'd mentioned Tracie, the Cockney girl we'd met under the statue of Eros in Piccadilly Circus. It was Froggie who first chatted her up, but she'd shot him down in forthright Cockney: 'Ge' off! Yah've eyes like Mor'y Feldman!'

He'd frowned at her, his eyes huge and quizzical. 'Who's Marty Feldman?'

His elbow thumped my ribs. 'Who's Marty Feldman?'

'Beats me, Froggie.' I returned to my quarter-pounder.

His big eyes fixed on Tracie – not directly, because Froggie's eyes are all askew, one looking north-west, the other south-east – but I saw that little glimmer glazing over the eyeballs that so strongly resembled egg-whites, that wet look that told me he'd been hurt and badly wanted to do something about Tracie's pretty looks.

I thought she'd up and split, but she just sat there, staring right back at him as the tension built up thick and strong. I made sure the burger held my exclusive attention.

Finally Froggie got up and sauntered over to a kid with spiky hair, a skinny fidgety kid who'd just taken some speed. 'Hey, pal,' Froggie asked him, 'did yeh ever hear o' Marty Feldman?'

The kid looked up. His pupils were huge, frantic and wary, and his right hand was trembling badly. Next he was on his feet and gone, risking sudden death by red bus or black curvy cab.

Froggie scowled after him and returned to the steps. 'Who's Marty Feldman, anyway?' he asked.

Tracie giggled behind one hand. Froggie's eyes grew huge

and murderous. Abruptly he turned away and was bounding down the steps. 'Pain in me arse stallin' around here. See yeh back at the flat, right?'

He pulled the wrap-around shades from his shirt pocket and put them on. 'Nice meetin' yeh, Trace. Keep goin' to the charm school, yeah?'

Tracie was a chatterbox. 'Dublin? Blimey! How do yah live there with all them army vans and bombs going off?'

'That's Belfast. We don't get tha' in Dublin.'

'Gor, your mate ain't 'alf ugly.'

'Shurrup. 'E's sound.'

I should have defended him better. After all, Froggie's a pal, a fellow Coolockian.

'Oi, foncy meetin' up tomorra? On yer own?'

I should've said no.

But by then I'd gotten a good view of cleavage.

I ran the razor over my face, splashed on the Brut and stuffed three twenties in my sky rocket. Froggie was sitting on the sofa, slicing up lead with the Stanley.

'Bad idea,' I told him. 'Maybe we should knock it on the head for a while, yeah? I mean, now that we're newsworthy.'

Froggie didn't look up. 'Fucked if I'm gonna sit cooped in this dive all night. Coupla heads goin' to Leicester Square later for a few bevvies. See yeh later. Tell fuck-face I wasn't askin' for her.'

I stood in the doorway. 'Froggie, you don't need to do the machines. I'll give yeh a score if yeh need it.'

'Yeh smell like a hoor's handbag.' He exploded with laughter. 'Tracie's handbag!'

'Come on. Been boozin' together since we left Dublin. Give us a bit of leeway, yeah?'

He waved a hand in the air. 'Go on, yeh treacherous bollocks.'

I hesitated at the door. 'Tell yeh what. We'll leave the city for a while, do the machines down in Brighton or somethin', yeah?'

He smiled up at me. Froggie might have gammy eyes, but his smile could torch the town, make a second great fire of London.

'Sounds good, Sundance.'

And that was the last time I saw him.

Seven o' clock became eight, eight pushed on to nine and at ten the neon signs flickered on – the big Coca-Cola sign, the ad for JVC video, the Sanyo illumination pulsing light up Shaftesbury Avenue. Tracie was obviously a woman with options.

They snared Froggie at Elephant and Castle tube station. Pockets stuffed with lead coins, probably why they nicked him so easily. Two coppers who might look handsome today, if only they'd thought twice about slagging Froggie off in the paddywagon. Froggie whipped out the Stanley and did some engraving on their faces. I remember something he once said: 'A dyin' art, face engravin'. Isn' it poxy the way the old skills're disappearin'?'

Magistrate packed him off to the Scrubs. I hear he's learned new skills. Mainlining's one of them. Funny thing, that. Froggie never touched gear outside of the nick.

Back in Dublin I souped up my CV and got a steady eddie number sitting at a computer terminal. I make a lot of tenpennies now, though I don't need to spend hours making them lead jackets.

Word around Coolock is Froggie was up for parole, but fucked up when a screw called him Marty. To be honest the story sounds too way out to be true … but you never know with the Frog. Apparently he got hold of some toothpicks and used one to pluck out the screw's eyes, just the same way you'd jab your stick into a cocktail sausage. Screw's eyes were left on the cell windowsill for the magpies. Word is Froggie's lost it and spends his days strapped in a giggle jacket.

Should've stayed with him. Got in a few cans, stuck on Muddy Waters; Froggie loosening up, telling me his dreams, splitting my sides as he slagged himself, rolling his eyes and making them swell till I thought they'd pop and shoot eyeball juice. Laughing and bantering in his Bogart voice, 'Here's lookin' at you, kid,' as his eyes struggled hard to bust out his head.

Lookin' back at yeh, Frog.

Kieran Byrne continues to publish stories and opinion pieces in such publications as the *Evening Herald*.

2001

EXPOSÉ

June Considine

Dublin-born June Considine is widely published as a writer of teenage fiction. Her best known titles are the *Luvender* and *Beechwood* series. This is her first published adult fiction. (2001)

We met for the first time in Planting Thought. I was in the rose garden pruning old wood from the ramblers when I glanced up and met his gaze. Dark eyes, speculative, so instantly familiar that it took a moment to realise we had never met. He looked just as intimidating as he did on television but his laughter had an easy sound as we discussed the miniature varieties of rose most suitable for growing in a small balcony space.

'What is it like to have the power to destroy people?' I asked before he left.

'People can only be destroyed if they have something to hide.' He cupped his hand under a rose and bent his head. Perhaps he wanted to breathe a different scent instead of sniffing in the footprints of other peoples' sins. The petals were fading, spread-eagled and as blowsy as a vulgar lady in red.

As an investigative journalist Greg Enright uncovered secrets. His research could snap a man's life in two and if, after an *Elucidate* exposé, a marriage broke up, a career ended, a nervous breakdown or heart attack occurred, that was not his concern. His job was to lift the stones and let the worms wriggle where they would. If that was wielding power, then so be it. He accepted it without being moved, intimidated or suppressed by his responsibilities.

He had driven to Malahide on a hunch – a trail that had ended in a cul-de-sac – and he was heading towards the M50 when he noticed the sign for Planting Thoughts. On that sunny afternoon a dead-end story no longer mattered. The real story was about to begin.

In a one-bedroom apartment on the high cobbles of the old Liberties, with Christ Church Cathedral behind and the sweep down to the Liffey in front, he lived alone. He had his music, his books, his workstation, a futon and a stream-lined kitchen where he loved to cook. His future on television was clearly traced on an upwardly mobile graft. He wanted to know everything about me. What was there to tell? I did not rip lives apart or terrify politicians. When I thought of television, it was to dream of hosting my own programme, designing fantastic gardens against impossible odds. Reality, however, was dirt under my fingernails and long sessions in Planting Thoughts, selling geraniums, marigolds and petunias.

Six months later we decided to marry. It seemed an inevitable progression. A declaration of permanent intent.

Maria, my cousin and cradle buddy, demanded to know if I was crazy, terminally ill from a wasting disease or pregnant. She called into Planting Thoughts one lunch hour to remonstrate. Why tie the knot, she demanded, perching on an upturned terracotta pot, when we had the option of living in sin and keeping spice in our lives.

She clicked her fingers in my face and ordered me to get a grip. I had fallen in love with a guy who was probably a member of the Inquisition in a former life. So what if he had a terrific dick, she demanded. Terrific dicks were ten a penny if I looked in the right places. It was a dismal excuse for marriage. I was rapidly regretting the indiscreet secrets I had confided in my cousin's willing ear.

'Greg is not the marrying kind,' she stated. This was a loaded comment, backed by insider information.

I concentrated on the climatic plants I was staking and ordered her to dish the dirt. She fulminated for a while before throwing the name of Carol Wynne at me. I shrugged it aside, becoming angry. But being angry with Maria is a lost cause. She simply ignores it, waiting until the emotion is exhausted before returning to her original point. I fixed my attention on the trailing stems. A plant with tentacles that would take over someone's garden, gripping tree trunks, wrapping around branches and clothes lines, embracing everything in its path. Like my love for Greg, entwined in my future, no matter what my cousin told me.

Carol Wynne was part of the *Elucidate* camera team, nifty on her feet when they did door-stepping features, sharing his excitement, the thrill of the chase. Their relationship never had a shape, easy to take up and put down again, no demands.

'She's dead wood,' I told Maria who groaned, demanding to be spared the horticultural metaphors. At the riding school where she worked, Carol Wynne was one of her pupils. If we were going to be metaphorical about it, then Maria was forced to declare that the lady in question had a tight grip once she got a horse between her knees.

I hauled her to her feet. I knew Greg Enright's secrets and he knew mine. Maria would be my bridesmaid, a vision in lilac.

I moved into his apartment after our wedding. At night we made love and slept exhausted, waking the following morning to consume each other again. His friends from *Elucidate* came to dinner. They filled the apartment with smoke and snide hot air. Carol Wynne touched our furniture with familiar hands.

'I believe you arrange flowers,' she said. A remark not exactly designed to inspire love. She asked for advice about her yucca plant in case I felt excluded from the conversations about political manoeuvrings and who was sleeping with whom on the coalition benches.

When my husband began to pursue Michael Hannon I felt a fleeting pity for the politician. Michael Hannon was the new, informed face of the far Right, a witty and articulate man. A polished television performer. He did not rant or make emotive statements. Nor did he invade family planning clinics or carry posters of dead foetuses. When he appeared on RTÉ he spoke in measured tones about the rights of the unborn, the dispossessed by divorce, the breakers of moral standards, the assault on the traditional values of family life. He was grooming himself for a ministerial position when the party he represented, Democracy in Action, was asked to form a coalition.

'We have the policies to lead this great nation into a new millennium,' he said. His ability to milk a platitude and make it sound genuine was a skill Greg could not help but admire. He had no problem with the views the politician espoused and would have been equally committed to exposing him if he had preached abortion on demand or the granting of divorce after walking three times backwards around Dáil Éireann. What Greg exposed was hypocrisy and if Michael Hannon's anthem was 'God Save Our Gracious Family' then he had no right to be in Portugal in a discreet hotel on top of a discreet mountain indulging in a discreet indiscretion with his wife's best friend.

When her husband spoke in public, a social smile sat like armour on Rachel Hannon's face. A rumour, too vague to be taken seriously but floating among journalists for years, hinted that she was a battered wife. Not the kind of wife who sought barring orders and displayed her bruises as evidence to sympathetic judges. Her bruises, if they existed, were hidden behind chic designer suits and butterfly smiles that sometimes distorted her mouth into a grimace.

It was suggested by those who dabbled with the story that after the cut and thrust of politics, the blood letting and vigorous debate, frustrations needed an outlet. Nothing had ever been proved. Journalists who tried to investigate found themselves facing a wall of denial from anyone they contacted. Editors, imagining libel suits and early retirement without pensions, refused to touch it. Even the producer on *Elucidate*, a tenacious pursuer of liars and knaves, was adamant. If Greg presented her with broken bones she would give them full disclosure. But anything else, forget it. *Elucidate* sailed close to the wind but was not in the business of self-destruction.

Anonymous tip-offs were a regular feature in Greg's life. I grew used to him hanging out in empty car parks and in the basements of inner city pubs, terrified when he was late home, imagining him nursing his own broken bones or worse. Sometimes he got lucky. When the anonymous note with the name of the politician and that of a woman, Gemma Kennedy, arrived through our letterbox one morning, he was exhilarated. It contained a date and the address of a Portuguese hotel. We had no trouble guessing the identity of the sender. Political destruction as compensation for domestic brutality. He showed the note to his producer who looked at it for a moment before ordering him to pack his sunscreen lotion. She was booking him and Carol Wynne on a flight to Portugal.

I told him we'd be fine on our own. 'Don't worry ... you can't not go,' I said, uttering wifely reassurances. Apart from the necessity of following the Hannon story to its conclusion, I knew he would appreciate escaping for a short time from the domestic reality of a three-month-old baby. Night feeds, nappy changes, colic, windy smiles. Enchantment, chaos.

At the airport Fay encircled his finger with her tiny fist and gazed around with startled eyes when the imminent departure of his flight was announced.

'Marital bliss,' murmured Carol Wynne. 'Where would you be without it. Just wait till you're a daddy of ten.'

He rented a car at Oporto Airport and drove towards the Serra do Caramulo. Trucks and juggernauts laboured up the steep inclines as the countryside fell away into forests of olive trees and eucalyptus. In my mind I can see those narrow mountainous roads and the green tangled vines shadowing the doorways of dusty farmhouses.

Breakfast was the perfect time to doorstep, they decided. Who could dispute the evidence of a pot of marmalade on the table? I imagine their excitement and how it evoked memories of other occasions when they had hunkered down together on the edge of breaking a story.

Night falls swiftly in Portugal and it was dark when they reached the hotel, the foyer as deserted as they had hoped.

Before he left, Greg had confessed his fear that they were on a fool's errant, depending on nothing more substantial than an anonymous tip-off. On top of a remote mountain, tired and anxious, it seemed a distinct possibility.

He rang me as soon as he showered. His room had tapestries of sailing ships and marble tiles that followed the flow of the sea. The line was bad, breaking off at times, and I had to shout that I missed him. I heard his voice, faint but clear, repeating the same words back to me.

When he awoke the following morning he stood on the balcony of his hotel room. Mist drifted over the lower hills. A grove of lemon trees edged the terraced fields like black serrated knives. Birds sang – trills and trebles – and Carole Wynne, her voice petulant, ordered him to close the balcony door on the dawn chorus.

Aerobics on a mattress. That was his description. Un-expected yet inevitable from the moment she came into his room with a bottle of vodka. They had talked of other times, recalling the intimacy of other hotel rooms and shared meals in cities where they were strangers, walking free. Laden memories, stirring a slow, responsive desire, and he pulled her close, feeling the familiar curves of her body, her mouth opening, seeking him. In those early moments I'm sure he thought about me with a shamed sense of guilt and then not at all, his excitement heightened by the knowledge that Michael Hannon was enjoying the same swamping pleasure in a room above them, unaware that retribution was at hand.

I hear their voices murmuring, sighing, moaning. In the white light of a Portuguese morning I see her copper hair swinging free as she smiles up at him. I picture my husband, steady and righteous, demanding that she erase last night's passion from her mind. Amnesia of the senses. Her smile fades. She is angry, ready for battle. She often wondered about his definition of fidelity. Now she knows. He carefully settles the sheet around her bare shoulders. Greg does not like distractions when he has a point to argue. He apologises for hurting her. He is impatient to shower and move in for the kill. A clear head is necessary, incisive questions, the full-frontal attack. She insists there is no need for apologies. He has never pretended to be anything other than an ambitious and selfish prick. If his wife throws him out and he is looking for a spare bed he is welcome to look in any direction … except hers. These are the words he laid before me, humbly, hoping I would find relief in her odium, in his shame.

Why do men insist on confession. I had no desire to be the wife who was the last to know. I did not want to know at all. Indiscretions can be absolved by time and silence. Guilt, on the other hand, is a heavy burden. Those who are not strong in their respect to keep their secrets have a need to share this guilt. To cast it aside through the seeking of forgiveness. In a previous era, Greg would have breathed his sins into the ear of a weary priest. He would have received a rosary as penance, recited slowly and with feeling. I would have received flowers and attention. Perhaps even a fur coat, depending on the nature of the indiscretion, and worn it proudly because in the good old days it was not considered necessary to empathise with the suffering of skinned animals. Instead I – wife, priest, psychologist – got the truth.

Michael Hannon and his companion dined on chilled fruit and cheeses, cold meats and crusty bread rolls. He murmured something and she laughed, inclining her head towards him. She noticed them first. Her face froze, her smile trapped as they advanced. She stretched out her hand to warn him. It hung motionless between them.

Carole Wynne sighed, her camera primed. 'He is a

handsome bastard,' she muttered. 'Such a shame to banish him for life from our television screens.'

'Is this your definition of family values, Mr Hannon?' my husband demanded. Like Michael Hannon, Greg has been known to milk a platitude or two when under duress. Lime flavoured marmalade, he noticed, as he thrust his microphone forward to catch the politician's muffled curse, the crash of an overturned chair. It was over in minutes.

As they drove down the winding roads of the Serra do Caramulo, the mist cleared. An aluminium sun shone low in the sky, as hard and bright as a newly minted coin. Greg wondered if his heart was large enough to entertain pity for the shattered ambitions of Michael Hannon. He wanted to believe it did. He knew it did not.

These days, Michael Hannon is a regular guest on current affairs programmes. He has purged his contempt for family values, and insider sources hint that the party is ready to welcome him back to the fold. I saw him recently at an opening night in the Abbey Theatre. Rachel Hannon's gaze drifted in my direction, then away again. She was much praised for her dignity, her courage under fire. If she had bruises they were still invisible. Her husband placed his arm around her shoulders and escorted her to her seat.

I followed behind, alone. The truth is only a bitch when it is exposed.

Since this story first appeared, June Considine has published two highly acclaimed and bestselling novels for adults with New Island, *When the Bough Breaks* and *Deceptions*.

MOTHERS

Deirdre Nally

Deirdre Nally was born in Dublin and now
lives in Rathfarnham. She has published
articles in various papers and magazines.
Following a creative writing course in
1998 she became a member of Ashfield
Writers' Group. Her first published story,
'Making Up', was short-listed for last
year's Hennessy Awards. (2001)

It was February and my grandmother had unearthed the Christmas decorations from under the stairs
and was busily pinning crêpe-paper
bells to the walls, balancing plastic
reindeers on top of the television set.
'Oh, take them down when she's not
looking,' my mother said, flying out
the door, books bulging out of her
straw bag, a crocheted shawl thrown
across her shoulder. She was doing an
evening degree course, catching the
seventeen bus to Belfield four nights a
week, leaving us to fend for ourselves,
look after our grandmother.

'Isn't she great, your mother,' the neighbouring women would say disapprovingly, as they mashed up mounds of potato and drained steaming vegetables at the sink.

My mother didn't cook dinners, she left notes. 'Cheese in fridge. Cut off blue bits and have on toast' or 'Heat up rest of beans in large tin. Leave some for me.'

We obeyed these notes, standing on chairs to peer into saucepans, stirring things with knives and fork handles and old knitting needles left lying around, running next door with can openers or jars we couldn't get the lids off of.

Our granny's minding us, we would blandly answer the neighbours as they wrenched the top off a bottle of brown sauce or cut the cellophane away from a packet of Easi-Singles. Our granny whom we had left sitting on the stairs, one stocking on, one stocking off, searching the atlas for Hong Kong where she planned to go on holidays next week.

'Can we come too?' we would say. 'Where's your pass-port? You can't go to Hong Kong without your passport.'

'Don't be teasing her.' My mother would arrive home from the university, cold after standing on campus for forty minutes waiting for the bus. She would unzip her boots and curl up on the couch, eating a large bowl of butterscotch Angel Delight or a Bovril sandwich, her crocheted shawl wrapped around her feet. My mother always seemed to be shivering in those days, her hands cupped around hot mugs, her shoulders hunched beneath huge cardigans and old blankets.

We only had one heater in the house, a two-bar electric that my grandmother insisted on taking up to bed with her. 'It's mine,' she would whinge, her bottom lip trembling like a child's. My mother would have to stay awake until the early hours of the morning before creeping into the bedroom to switch it off. My mother had dark rings permanently etched beneath her eyes and red chipped nails chewed to the quick.

My grandmother went to a centre during the day where everyone made paper flowers and played bingo and sat around singing 'Row, row, row your boat, Gently down the stream', clapping their hands in time. My grandmother would confuse the issue by suddenly breaking into 'We all live in a yellow submarine' or 'Up, up and away in my beautiful balloon'. She would tear up the occupational therapist's paper roses, scattering them around the room chanting, 'I'm a flower girl, I'm a flower girl,' and shout 'House' at bingo every two minutes, without bothering to mark her card. My mother hated leaving her there.

It meant, however, that we could go to school and my mother could go to work in the County Council office where she had a supervisor called Sheila who put red x's beside the names of anyone who signed in late and told my mother her cheesecloth dresses and leather bracelets were not appropriate attire for a clerk of the local government.

My mother was always planning what she was going to say to Sheila when she finished her degree and was finally able to walk down the green linoed corridor and out through the heavy wooden doors for the very last time.

And after she had planned what she would say she would take out her psychology books and spread them around the kitchen table, studying and studying until three and four in the morning, shadows darkening beneath her eyes.

My mother had great plans for when she got her degree. Sometimes on a Sunday afternoon we would go walking, her and I, leaving my sister and grandmother at home watching *Little House on the Prairie*. We would stroll around Dartry on the damp wintry afternoons, the wind leaving a wet bloom on our faces as we looked at the red brick houses with the gravel drives and the white window frames and the huge trees growing in the front gardens.

'When I'm a psychologist,' my mother would say, 'we'll have a house like that.'

'With a bedroom of my own?' I would ask.

'With three bedrooms of your own,' she would say, tossing back her hair, and we would link arms and run to the nearest sweet shop to buy my grandmother's favourite bars of Fry's Chocolate Cream.

My grandmother nearly electrocuted herself one evening, plugging the hoover in to the plughole behind the fridge and dragging it out into the wet back yard to clear up the leaves while my sister and I fought upstairs over a torn *Bunty* annual. My mother got home just as blue sparks were beginning to flash from the flex as it tore away from the plug.

Another evening she was met by the sight of my grandmother sitting on the garden wall convinced she was waiting for the bus. 'It's very late,' she kept saying. 'I've got to be there by five.' It was ten o'clock at night and she was wearing just a nightdress and a single pink roller in her hair.

My mother began to skip her lectures after that, staying at home, frying us chips and heating up tins of spaghetti, steering my grandmother away from sockets and gas rings and unlocked front doors.

When we were all in bed she would take out her psychology texts and read and read, desperate to make up for lost time. Sometimes in the morning she would still be there, her eyes closed, her hair tumbled forward, her cheek crumpling the flimsy pages of last night's book.

She began to get more and more red x's after her name and eventually a talking to from Sheila who told her that her increment was in jeopardy if things didn't improve.

'It means I mightn't get my pay rise,' she explained, slumped on the couch, cradling a mug of Nescafé.

'Who needs a pay rise,' I said, walking on my hands across the balding carpet.

My mother sighed and pulled another piece of foam from the arm of the sofa.

The old people's home was called St Benedict's, written in an arch on the bubbled glass over the front door. We packed her belongings into bin liners and splashed out on a taxi, my sister, my mother, my grandmother and me. The taxi driver hummed along to 'Tie a yellow ribbon round the old oak tree' on the radio and told my mother about his brother-in-law's accident with a lawnmower.

My grandmother was to have a room at the back of the house, shared with one other person, the beds divided by flowery plastic curtains. She had a locker and a bedside chair of her own, but the wardrobe was shared.

Downstairs in the residents' lounge a television on a high shelf blared an old black and white western at the audience who slumped in their chairs, feet bulging shapelessly out of slippers, ketchup and medicine staining their cardigans.

'A hairdresser comes in on Tuesdays,' the matron told my mother. 'And the folk group give us half an hour on a Thursday evening. Baths are between seven and eight. Twice a week per resident.' The week's menus were pinned to a notice board in the hall. A pile of tatty magazines sat on a table. A fat woman with bulging arms, draped in a white butcher's apron, bustled in and out of a swing door marked 'kitchen'.

My grandmother clutched a green ashtray that she had insisted on taking from the mantelpiece at home. It was shaped like a square, the rim dipping and curving unevenly. She grasped it so tightly I thought it would break.

'I think we'd better go home now,' she said. 'It's starting to get dark.' And she held on to the ashtray with both hands.

We caught the bus home, carrying a bin liner each, ignoring the bus conductor's sighs every time he tripped over them in the aisle. My grandmother hummed 'Row, row, row your boat', rubbing her finger round and round the edge of the ashtray.

My mother drew squiggles on the steamed-up window, her finger moving aimlessly across the glass. Occasionally she stopped to chew on a red bitten nail as her eyes stared through the big old houses in Dartry. The ones where we were going to live some day, when she was a famous psychologist.

Deirdre Nally is currently working on a collection of short stories.

REUNION

Karen Gillece

Karen Gillece was born in Dublin. She studied Law at UCD, lived in London and Belgium for a while and is now an IT project manager in Dublin. She was encouraged to write by Mary O'Donnell at a creative writing course at the Irish Writers' Centre. *Reunion* is her first published fiction. (2001)

He slides into the seat opposite me, pulling off his hat and signalling to the waitress for service. I stop stirring my tea and look up and smile. We are sitting in the window seat of a café called Partners. The irony does not escape him.

'Partners, huh?' he laughs nervously.

The waitress approaches and he orders a double espresso and a sticky bun. She looks at me.

'Nothing for me, thanks. I'm fine,' I say.

'So?'

'So.'

'So how's work? How's the flat?'

'Fine, it's grand. Everything's fine. And you?'

'Oh, you know,' he shrugs.

This is the third time we've met in the eighteen months since we parted. That's if you don't count that Thursday evening in Sainsbury's when we passed at the fruit and veg counter but pretended not to see each other. He became engrossed in a watermelon, prodding and sniffing it, while I scurried past with my trolley. I haven't shopped there since.

'Did you get that gutter sorted out?' he asks. 'Because I was thinking that in weather like this you'd need to get it fixed.'

My gaze is drawn to the window. The rain is coursing down in uneven sheets.

'It's fixed.'

'Good. Good.'

His order arrives and he begins adding sugar and stirring, unfolding napkins and sorting out the cutlery. I follow the movements of his hands as he lays everything out in their proper order. He always was methodical.

I remember when we first moved into the flat, we didn't have a table so we improvised, using a big wooden crate instead. Every evening he would cover it with a tablecloth and set a place for each of us with pepper, salt and a jug of water or bottle of wine in between. I remember he couldn't bear to have ketchup bottles or cartons of milk on the table. The clutter jarred with him.

The crate didn't last very long. It had begun to dip in the middle so that our plates would keep slipping towards the centre. So one Saturday afternoon in May, we went to a car-boot sale in Streatham. It was the first car-boot sale I had ever been to. I'm not quite sure what I was expecting but what I got was a small patch of wasteland that was referred to as 'The Common', which was littered with forlorn pieces of furniture. Not a car-boot in sight.

It was being run by an old man called Gus who had a white bristly beard and a huge beer-gut hanging over his trousers.

'Dirty old geezer,' Dave said.

Dave came with the two of us to Streatham that day.

'Just to keep you company,' he said. 'Can't have you two going mad with your money. Someone has to keep an eye on the pennies.'

Now that I come to think back on it, Dave spent a lot of time with us those first few months. He practically lived on our sofa. There's still a whiff of cigarettes, alcohol and cheap cologne off it, which reminds me of him. But that was before he went to Australia in search of a better life, or at least 'the same lousy life but with sunshine and a tan'. The last I heard of him was a postcard written in some haste from a remote part of Queensland:

'G'day! I'm throwing a snag on the Barbie for ya! Still missing that sofa of yours, Dave.'

We bought a very sad and pathetic little table in the end. It was just a piece of chipboard covered in cheap blue lino, balanced precariously on four very unsteady legs. We tied it to the roof-rack and brought it home. I loved that table. It was the first thing we bought together. A corner of the lino peeled away and in a fit of childish romance, I scribbled our initials underneath on the rotting chipboard. I'm sure that they're still there. There have been nights since that I would gladly have hacked them away with a knife or a scissors. But somehow they have survived, immortalised forever.

He looks different somehow; I can't put my finger on it. Physically he hasn't changed, but there's something about his air or manner that wasn't there before. He reminds me of a small child wearing new clothes, all careful and upright and proud. He wasn't like that before.

I'm tearing up serviettes now while half-listening to his

conversation. This is a nervous habit I have. My hands need to be occupied constantly. I used to smoke. That was great – my hands had a ball but my lungs weren't too happy. I never became addicted to the actual inhalation part of smoking, just the handling part. After I left school, I grew my nails really long and my friend Alison filed and painted them for me. They looked terrific. I used to practise dragging on my Silk Cut Blues, letting the smoke curl out of my mouth, and then I would tap the ash into the ashtray with those gorgeous talons. It was pure sex.

'I'm getting married.'

My mind has been drifting in and out of this conversation but now it firmly takes root on this statement.

'I'm getting married,' he repeats, in case I hadn't heard him properly the first time.

'Oh,' I say. It's amazing how much meaning can be packed into one short syllable. I force a smile that I don't feel.

'Congratulations!'

He looks doubtful. I try harder.

'Really, that's brilliant news.' My jaw is aching with the effort. This second, braver attempt is more successful.

'Do you mean that?'

'Of course I do! I'm thrilled for you.'

He exhales and relaxes in his seat smiling.

'Oh good. I was worried that you'd be ... well ... but you're not, so ...'

I'm not a very good liar but I'm good enough to fool him.

He's telling me about her now. She's called Laura. They met at some garden party or barbecue. She teaches children with learning difficulties. How can I compete with one so noble?

I'm drifting away again. I don't want to hear anything about her, this new recipient of his love. I used to spend hours, whole afternoons wondering what it would be like to be married to him. I even flicked through a few bridal magazines to extend my fantasy.

But there was never any real danger of him becoming my husband. In the three years of my life that I spent with him we only discussed it once. It was during the World Cup after Ireland had beaten Italy. It was so hot that night in London. The heat seemed to wrap itself around us in great clammy blankets. The drink was flowing fast and freely in The Swan and after a while the heat went unnoticed. Stumbling out into the hot night, we had stopped a mini-cab and slid onto the backseat. We found our way home to the flat, clambered over Dave on the sofa, deep in beer-sodden slumber. I threw open the window in our bedroom, allowing some of the heat to escape, and then I lay down on the bed next to him.

He kissed my face and my neck, pushing my hair away.

'I love you, you know that don't you?' he whispered. 'I mean I really love you.'

The tinge of sweat and alcohol from his skin was intoxicating. He fumbled with my clothes, lifting and tugging with a new immediacy, becoming more excited while I stroked his back, soothing and slow. We made love under a cloud of sultry heat; it was fast and exhilarating, like speeding through the desert in an open-top car. Afterwards, as we lay together in the darkness, drifting into sleep, he said it to me.

'I'm going to marry you.'

I remember those words clearly. The sound of Dave snoring in the next room, the gentle hum of the sleeping city and those words hanging suspended in the air.

'I'm going to marry you.'

And then that rush of emotion, more potent than any alcohol or illegal substance that I had ever known, sweeping over me, throbbing and immediate. It was suffocating. I thought I would drown in it.

That was the last time we ever spoke about marriage. He

didn't mention it the next morning as he nursed his hangover, or the morning after that, or the morning after that.

The rain is petering out as we leave the café. I put up my umbrella anyway and he pulls on his hat. A large raindrop hits his cheek and he wipes it away with the back of his hand. We turn and face each other.

'So.'

'So.'

He leans down and brushes my forehead with a kiss.

'Take care of yourself, hmm?'

'I will. You too.'

'Good luck.'

'Bye.'

'Bye.'

I turn away and head down the street towards the tube station. I pull my coat tightly about myself and drive forward, my head bent, leaning into the wind.

Karen Gillece's first novel, *Seven Nights in Zaragoza*, was published by Hodder Headline Ireland in February 2005 to critical acclaim and has been translated into several European languages. Her second novel, *Longshore Drift*, is due to be published in February 2006.

2002

TABLE FOR TWO

Moyra Donaldson

Moyra Donaldson is a poet, editor and creative writing tutor whose first poetry collection, *Snakeskin Stilettos*, was published to critical acclaim by Lagan Press in Ireland and by Cavankerry Press in America, where it was short-listed for a Foreword Book of the Year Award. Her second collection, *Beneath the Ice*, was published by Lagan Press in December 2001. A founding member of the Creative Writers' Network and its current co-chair, and a previous Literary Editor for *Fortnight Magazine*, she has edited a number of anthologies, including *Down at the Millennium* and *Alchemy*. She was awarded an Arts Council Award in 2001 and in the same year received the Artist of the Year Award from Belfast City Council, working within the Chinese community. (2002)

Despite his coaxing, she didn't want to go. Her eyes remained fixed on the television and, watching the picture flicker in her pupils, he felt a kind of desperation overtake him. He tried again. 'You'd enjoy it, I hear it's really nice, lots of seafood.' She shook her head. 'I've told you – I don't feel like it.'

Finally he phoned the restaurant anyway, and waited, feeling like a conspirator, while a professionally polite young man on the other end checked to see if a table was available. Yes, but only if they could be there by eight thirty. He checked his watch: just 40 minutes to get ready and to drive the fifteen miles along the twisting coast road. The theme tune of a game show seeped round the closed living room door and into his consciousness. She must have turned it up. 'We'll be there,' he said. 'A table for two.'

She didn't argue as he'd expected her to, but got up slowly, sighing as she went upstairs to change. He clicked off the television with a satisfied flourish of the remote and followed her up. 'Don't take too long now,' he said, as she opened the wardrobe door. In the bathroom he ran the electric razor over his chin then checked himself in the mirror. Not bad, he thought, not too bad. He took a quick piss so he wouldn't get caught short in the car, then washed his hands and went back into the bedroom. She was sitting, dressed only in her bra and knickers, still as an island in the chaotic sea of clothes that covered the bed. He looked at his watch. 'All right, I know,' she said. 'I just can't find anything I feel right in.' He picked up a dress at random. 'This one. You look great in this one.' For a strange suspended moment, he thought she was going to hit him, then she took the dress from his hands and slipped it over her head. He felt off balance, as if something had shifted under his feet, then shifted back again, too quickly for him even to be sure it had happened. She stood, letting the dress fall over her hips, then turned her back to him. 'Zip me up, would you?'

He smoked two cigarettes while she put on her make-up. He didn't really want the second, but it was something to do while he waited. If she sensed his impatience it made no difference; her face in the mirror of the powder compact was a miniature of concentration. He watched as she tilted her chin this way and that, as if trying to catch sight of something just out of frame. By the time he was backing the car out of the garage they had twenty minutes left to get there.

It was a lovely evening, after such a heavy, overcast day. The late sun stained the lough pink and three windsurfers skidded across the waves, their sails the yellow and blue of tropical butterfly wings. The conjured image pleased him and as he watched one board leapt into the air as if trying to take flight, surf the sky. He smiled as he pressed his foot down on the accelerator. It was good to be out of the house. 'It's a lovely evening,' he said.

'Yes, it is.' She stretched out her legs, relaxing down into her seat. 'You forget how nice it is down this way.' He reached over and pressed her knee and she laid her hand on his, left it there.

Round the next corner, he had to brake sharply behind a tractor and trailer, the trailer piled high with silage. He took his hand from beneath hers to change down into second. Damn, this was going to hold them up. He swerved out and in, trying to see if it was safe to pass, but with the road's tight bends, he couldn't see far enough to be sure. Wads of the ripe, bruised grass dropped onto the road in front of them as the trailer bumped and swayed and he could feel his tension rising again. Nebulous fears and forebodings. Don't, he thought, don't let yourself get stressed, it'll be OK. Suddenly a red BMW appeared in his rear view mirror, then, without slowing, swept on past, overtaking the tractor and trailer as well. One fast, easy manoeuvre. He only had time to catch a quick glimpse of its driver before it disappeared round the next bend. Flash bastard, he thought. Aloud, he said, 'He couldn't possibly have known the road was clear. Imagine if you were coming the other way, meeting a lunatic like that.' He could hear his own voice, high and indignant. Like an old man, he thought, like my father. He sensed her watching him as he drummed his fingers on the steering wheel, but he couldn't stop. His arms felt charged with static.

Half a mile further, where the road straightened briefly, he drew out, accelerated and overtook, pushing the car through the gears. He glanced down at his watch. Christ, he hated being late. Twenty-five past and they weren't even half way.

'Don't worry, they're not going to send us away again, even if we are a bit late.' He looked for sarcasm in her words, her tone, and finding none, felt his tension ebb again and the muscles in his arms and chest relax. She was right, he thought, so what if they weren't there exactly on time. He must stop getting things so out of proportion.

The next time he allowed himself to look at his watch, he'd already found a parking space and was waiting for her to close her door so that he could lock it. A quarter to, not too bad, still he hurried her up the street, only slowing as they reached the door. Inside, a waiter showed them into the small bar, more like a snug really, and asked what they'd like to drink. He hesitated. 'I'll drive,' she said, so he ordered a pint for himself and a Ballygowan for her; immediately he felt guilty. 'You can have a glass of wine with your meal sure,' he said and she nodded.

He clinked his glass to hers and drank the first half of the pint in one long swallow. He felt foolish now, being so up tight about getting there on time. There was no sense of rush at all in the restaurant, and the waiter didn't come back for ten minutes, by which time he was ready for another pint. The menu looked good and by the time the waiter came back again to show them to their seats, he'd decided on garlic mussels, followed by medallions of monkfish. She ordered a salad bowl of olives and feta cheese and a main course of salmon. The wine list was extensive and expensive and he felt a slight pang of anxiety. He was already a bit short. Too much month at the end of the salary, as he would quip in the office. God, he thought, how must I sound to the twenty-somethings with their sharp suits and sharper eyes. An old fogey.

Settling back in his chair he looked around. The walls were a pale sandwashed colour, and a huge picture window looked out onto the harbour where the ferry was just pulling away, its wake leaving some small yachts bobbing anxiously. He realised she was sitting with her back to the scene.

'Why don't you sit here,' he said. 'Then you can see out. It's a beautiful view.' He half rose, but she signalled with her napkin for him to sit back down.

'I'm OK as I am,' she said, and he heard the note of irritation in her voice.

He ordered an overpriced bottle of Chablis and surreptitiously took in the other diners. Mostly couples, middle aged and well groomed. There were no loud voices. Any laughter was polite and subdued. One table of six at the window seated what looked like three generations of the one family. A daughter who looked like her mother, who looked like her mother. Their respective men. A birthday celebration he guessed.

He was enjoying his food, enjoying being in the restaurant among other people. He felt part of the gentle flow of sociability and tried to lift her mood to his, starting conversations, telling her amusing stories from work. She said little in return, acknowledging his light banter with the tight little smiles that didn't get any further than her lips. She was disappointed with the salad. The olives were green and stuffed, not black as she said they should be really. The salmon was overdone. He poured what wine was left in the bottle into his glass.

'You've hardly touched yours,' he said.

'Too dry for my taste,' she said. 'I'll just have a coffee.'

'I might as well have it then.'

She shrugged. 'Go ahead, I don't want it.'

The family group was leaving, moving towards the door when it happened, as it sometimes would despite his best efforts. His imagination leapt from his control, and for an instant it was him, standing up, nodding and smiling, holding the door open for his daughter. Zoë. She'd have been thirty-two this year. He cleared his throat of the image and the choking sensation it brought, and at the same time accidentally caught the waiter's attention. Ordered coffee and a large brandy.

Outside the night had grown chilly and he felt the last of the warmth and *bonhomie* of the restaurant drain away. As he watched her unlock the car, a picture of a timer popped into his mind. He could see the tight waist of glass, the sand running through. Four years, he thought, four years of being a family. Nothing compared to the vast deserts of time since.

In the car he closed his eyes, trying to keep the encroaching headache from taking hold. He kept them closed, sensing rather than seeing the on-coming headlights on his eyelids, until he felt the car turn into their drive. 'Thanks for driving,' he said as she switched off the engine.

'I thought you were sleeping.'

'I'm sorry,' he said, 'I was just ...'

But before he could finish she'd opened the door and stepped out. He followed her into the house. 'I'm going on up,' she said, and he nodded.

She was taking off her make-up when he came into the bedroom. Her face was shiny and vulnerable in the light from the bedside lamp. He felt a sudden weight in his chest as if something was boring through it. Anti-matter, he found himself thinking. She set down the cotton wool she'd been using and popped her sleeping pill into her mouth, swallowed, then settled back against the pillow. She doesn't see me, he thought, she can't see me. The weight in his chest increased and he moved his hand in front of his face to check its solidity – then her eyes met his and he felt stupid. Still, it took his heart a while to settle back into its normal rhythm.

She waited until he'd undressed and got into bed before switching off the light. He felt her settle beside him, her back to his. 'Thanks for coming out with me tonight.' His voice sounded too loud in the dark. She wriggled over a little so that her buttocks touched his, and he imagined turning round to her, cupping her breasts in his hands. Instead he lay still, listened as her breath slowed towards sleep, and wondered if it was her loneliness or his own that made him want to weep.

In 2004 Moyra Donaldson received her second Arts Council Award. Her third collection of poetry, *The Hummingbird Case*, is forthcoming this year from Lagan Press and she is currently working on a book of short stories and a play.

THE SOLDIER'S SONG

Alan Monaghan

After leaving school, Alan Monaghan served an apprenticeship as a boilermaker in Guinness's brewery, and subsequently started his career as an engineer. He works in Dublin and his story 'Rosary' was short-listed for a Hennessy Award in 1995. (2002)

It is six o'clock on a winter's morning and the stars are still out. The still air is icy and sharp in my throat. As I march across the frosty cobbles, my breath streams out behind me like the smoke from a ship and the only sound is my footsteps echoing around the Barrack Square.

I haven't slept at all. I've still got the sour taste of cigarettes and whiskey in my mouth and my uniform reeks of turf from the little fire in the adjutant's office. It was a long night, full of things I thought I had forgotten, but now I can't help remembering. And one thing, one man, above all. I never even knew his name, but it's his face that haunts me now. When I poured the cold water for a shave in the adjutant's office I saw it in the mirror, staring at me. Just a glimpse, but long enough for one accusing look — as if he knew what I was about to do.

They must have been keeping watch for me. As I approach the door of the guardroom, I can hear them moving about inside. I barge into the meagre warmth and find the five of them on their feet, half-dressed and red-eyed with lack of sleep. I can see his face in every one of theirs and I feel ashamed to look at them: young country boys, straight out of school and still missing their mothers. And me in my brushed greatcoat, brass buttons and polished brown boots. Captain Reilly, of the Irish Free State Army. Then Mullarkey draws himself up and offers an uneasy salute, followed by the rest. They are soldiers after all. But I can't bring myself to return the salute. I just nod and take the minister's order from my pocket.

He had come out to France with a replacement draft and went straight to Dalton's platoon. There were so many replacements by then that it was hard to remember even the names of those in my own platoon. The only thing that set this one apart was when Dalton reported him missing at battalion headquarters the day after we went into the line. That was barely a week after he had arrived in France. But now Dalton was gone — hit in both legs by a machine-gun — and his missing man was back. They had picked him up six miles behind the lines with no rifle, no papers and an old peasant's overcoat over his uniform.

We all knew what must follow. Rumours of an execution had been whispered up and down the trenches for three days. Even a heavy German counterattack hadn't been able to silence them. At dawn we had marched out of the line, and now we were halted in the shade of an orchard with thick, soft grass growing around the trees and the scent of apple blossom hanging in the warm air. After the trenches, we felt we had

*escaped to another world. It was a fine summer morning and we lay
dead tired and scattered around the grass like corpses, listening to the
distant guns warming to their day's work. Whum, whum, whum, they
went, a roaring chorus.*

*A little apart from the others, four officers lay under a tree, smoking
cigarettes and passing around a hip flask. Four of us left out of the ten
who had gone into the line. And we could hardly have passed for officers;
grimy, unshaven and stinking of sulphur and sweat. There was very little
talk. We knew it wasn't finished yet.*

The gathering daylight is like the end of winter. It chases the
sugary frost into the corners, and shrinks the nighttime
expanse of the square down to four grey walls. I'm drilling the
five of them outside, with the sun rising in front of me; red
and angry, sliding slowly out of a crimson scar above the
rooftops. *Eos Rhododoktulos*, the rosy fingered dawn. Not the
sharpest squad I've ever seen, but the *as gaeilge* commands don't
come to me very easily. I ought to have a sergeant to drill
them, but there are rumours of discontent among the older
soldiers and the distant whiff of mutiny in the Free State's
infant army. They are growing tired of the fight, Irishman
against Irishman, and there have been too many executions
already. It's ironic, then, that this one should turn out to be
an Englishman, albeit a Sinn Féin Englishman; caught on the
run in Glendalough, with a pistol in his pocket.

So I bark my own commands, facing them with my
hands held behind my back and five rounds of ammunition
clenched in my fist. One round is blank, as required by the
regulations. I read them again last night, before I cleaned
and reloaded the heavy revolver on my hip. There are no
blanks in the revolver. My part will be certain, without even
the comfort of doubt.

In spite of myself, I snatch another glance at my
wristwatch. The time on the order has already passed, but I

know it's getting close because of the sun on my face. He's asked to see the sun one last time. *Eos Rhododoktulos* – her fingers dipped in blood. The same baleful red eye that watched vengeful Achilles fall on proud Hector. That's the trouble with education: it lets you put a name to every bloody thing.

A messenger came down from brigade HQ with a note for Captain Byrne. It was the warning we had been expecting. With a face like thunder, Byrne told Nugent to see if there were five men left from Dalton's platoon, and had the rest of us form ranks in the muddy field behind the orchard. This had last been used as an artillery paddock, and stank of horseshit, with clouds of shiny black flies buzzing around us where we stood. About a hundred of us left, standing in two ragged rows. The barrage was still going on up the line, in full flow now, rippling up and down the horizon like distant music. Out of the corner of my eye, I could see the man beside me; a grimy silhouette, hollowed and grey, like the face on a silver coin. But clearly alive, twitching imperceptibly with every detonation.

After a few minutes the noise stopped suddenly. It left a deep uncomfortable silence, like someone had lifted the needle off a gramophone record. But we all knew what was going on behind the silence. Men looked at each other knowingly. We were too far off to hear it but we knew; the fearful grunts and harsh exhortations; the stinging rifle cracks; the thud of metal into flesh; the merciless sewing machine clacking of a machine gun. The screams.

This is the place; a dingy gravel yard with no windows looking into it. It's very small and he's in here with us – taking a final turn around the yard with his clergyman. I find my eyes following him around. He's dressed in a neat tweed suit; shoes shined, and his tie done all the way up. Walking ramrod straight with his hands behind his back – just like a country gentleman out for his morning stroll. I don't think I could have managed it in his position. I wouldn't have been able for the tie.

Now he's shaken hands with the reverend and he's bearing down on me; blue eyes fixed on mine, probing for some sign of weakness. I force myself to meet his gaze as best I can.

'Good morning, Captain Reilly.' His voice is hard, clipped; his British accent prominent even in this short phrase. But there is a civil inclination to his head, and a faintly amused look in his eyes.

'Mr Childers,' I reply, taking his outstretched hand without thinking. His grip is hard and firm. I hope he doesn't see my hand trembling as I take it away.

'Good morning, lads,' he calls out to the squad, and then strides up to the line, his hand out. There is some awkward uncertainty, some nervous swallows, and I catch young Mullarkey looking to me for approval. I give a nod, and he takes Childers' hand, pumping it forcefully.

'Sir!' Mullarkey bellows, staring stiffly over Childers' shoulder. And so it continues down the line; wooden handshakes, eyes staring over the top of his head as he looks approvingly into their faces. There is a palpable sense of relief as he reaches the end of the line and walks back to me, hands safely behind his back once again.

'You'll forgive me for asking, Captain, but do we still have an agreement?'

'Well, I can't say I understand it, but I'm prepared to honour your request. Provided you don't take too long about it, of course.'

'No,' he laughed, 'No, of course not, Captain. I'll not delay, you have my word.'

'Very well then. My men will ready and aim on my command, but will only fire on yours.'

'Thank you, Captain.' He smiled. 'Well, in that case, I suppose we'd better get on with it.'

They brought him down the road in the back of a supply lorry. Four MPs in the back with him, and the colonel himself riding slowly behind on a big bay mare. Nobody was surprised to see him here. The colonel had been with the Dublins since the start and never shirked. Wounded at Le Cateau in the first days of the war, he went on to lose an eye in Gallipoli, and survived a second bullet at Ginchy. While the lorry squealed to a halt behind the ranks, the colonel wheeled his horse around to face us, the animal bucking and snorting at the scent of the previous occupants. His stern face and eye-patch overwhelmed the urge we all felt to crane our necks and get a closer look at the boy. For a moment he looked like he might speak to us, but he knew where we had been, and that there was nothing to say. He nodded sadly and looked to the men in the lorry.

'Well, get on with it then.'

The wall is embarrassing. It's covered with bullet holes; pocked and cratered from a dozen mornings before this one. They haven't even bothered to whitewash over it. Even more disquieting is the sound of normal life on the other side. Dublin City is coming awake and I can hear the cries of a milk cart, the clop-clop of horse's hooves and the rhythmic thud of somebody beating a carpet.

I've got a blindfold in my pocket, but he doesn't want it, which is just as well, because it wouldn't do to let him see how badly my hands are shaking. It's the best I can do to get the square of white cloth pinned to the breast of his jacket without stabbing him in the heart.

My mind isn't on the job. I'm trying to imagine myself somewhere else. During the worst times in France, I used to picture myself as a young boy, playing in the garden, or sitting in the kitchen with the smell of baking bread. Now it's more immediate; I've got one place I can return to. It's a place not far off: a bedroom with green curtains drawn. A slim figure curled up in the bed with the warm curve of her arm against the cool white sheets. Brown hair fanned across the pillow.

He's looking at me as I step backwards, that amused

look on his face again. I wish I could turn around now, and keep walking away.

'Do you believe in God, Captain?'

'Not for this long time.'

'We can agree on that much, at least.' He is holding out his hand to me again. 'Goodbye, Captain, and good luck.'

He struggled and writhed like an animal in a trap, but they formed a tight knot around him, moving purposefully across the grass with the prisoner in their midst. His head and shoulders bobbed urgently, as if he was drowning amongst them. The squad was forming up in front of the orchard wall. Craning his head back, he scanned the stony ranks, searching for some sign of hope. His eyes met mine for an instant, terrified and pleading at the same time. I looked away.

'Help me, lads!' he cried, his accent very plain, very young. 'They're going to shoot me, lads. Jesus, Mary and Joseph, will ye not help me? Will ye not help an Irish lad?'

'Where's your dignity, boy?' a gruff voice asked from behind me.

'Please!' he cried again, as they let him fall to his knees in front of the wall. Two of the MPs held him in that position while a third tied on his blindfold. 'Oh God help me, lads, they're going to murder me. I'm only sixteen, lads. I let on I was older.'

He choked on the last word and started crying uncontrollably. His resistance was gone. The MPs dragged him roughly upright and spun him around to face the squad. They let him fall then, leaning back against the wall. There was a spreading wet patch in the front of his trousers.

'God help us,' the man beside me whispered under his breath, blessing himself.

'Ready!' The order was spoken in a wavering voice. Nugent was as white as a sheet. Five rifle bolts were snapped shut and locked. The boy cocked his head to one side at the sound, turning it from side to side as if he was trying to see us through the blindfold. Time seemed to slow down and there was a long silence when the birds in the apple trees sang very clearly.

'Are ye still there, lads?'

'Take aim!'
   'Oh . . .' He started to sing, chin down, his high reedy voice cracking,
'Is it true what they say . . .'

'Fire!' The single word cracks out and a ragged volley kills it dead on his lips. I'm facing across the line of rifles, mouth clamped shut, eyes straight ahead. I can't see him, but I know he's there. I know what I'll see when I turn my head.

'Shoulder arms!' I shout into the rising cloud of blue smoke. I can hear the chaplain, clacking his beads and muttering in Latin.

I turn slowly and force my eyes down to the huddled figure. He looks smaller now than he did, I think, and start to walk forward, footsteps crunching loudly in the gravel. Up close he looks shabby; I can see the frayed collar of his shirt and the pockmarked skin on the nape of his neck, with downy hair blowing in the breeze. He is lying face down with one arm stretched out, his hand moving, clawing at the gravel. The revolver is heavy in my hand, the hammer hard under my thumb. There's a familiar face coming to the front of my mind, accusing, but I try to push it aside and cock the revolver with an effort. Brown hair fanned across the pillow.

'The Soldier's Song' won the Emerging Fiction prize as well as the overall Hennessy New Irish Writing Award and Alan Monaghan is currently finishing his first novel, also called *The Soldier's Song*.

Dancing Queen

Trudy Hayes

Trudy Hayes has published short stories
and play extracts in various publications
and anthologies, including *Virgins and
Hyacinths* (Attic Press) and *Irish Women:
Writings Past and Present* (Gill & Macmillan).
Her play *Out of My Head* was nominated for
the Stewart Parker Theatre Award, and her
play *Making Love to Yorrick* was staged in the
Dublin Fringe Festival 1998. She is author
of *The Politics of Seduction* (Attic Press). She
lives in Shankill, Co. Dublin. (2002)

I'm forty, big-bosomed, and I hope
there's a bit of life in me yet. I get
myself dolled up in my black vamp
dress, feathers ruffling around my
neck, and paint my fingernails with
blood-red polish and look sadly at
myself in the wardrobe mirror.

The dyed hair. Bright, ever-hope-
ful eyes look back at me, despite life's
hard knocks, the pointless optimism
that has carried me through life. I
wonder do I look sad, sad and fat

and forty. But men are still attracted to me. I still look a bit of stuff despite my slightly scattered look. My lost 'love me' eyes attract men, but a woman who doesn't know how to take care of herself has to take care. Men recognise the needy and the vulnerable, and they'll exploit you if they get a chance.

I'm going to Dance Macabre on Mount Street tonight, which is apparently for the over thirties, and I'm told you're bound to meet someone there. I'm going on my own, slightly ashamed of myself. I was there once with a friend and I tried to enjoy myself but she's gone on holidays to Greece. I just want to hear the pound of disco music again, feel once again that flicker of expectation, the desperate hope of meeting somebody that is probably more satisfying than any possible reality. My husband is asleep, drunk, downstairs on the sofa. I hope to God he doesn't leave the cooker on again and set the place on fire. I'm terrified. I came in last night and he was stretched on the floor, comatose. I can't bring any friends home now, can't risk it because I don't know what state he'll be in. Everybody's advising me to get a barring order.

I have to do something to save myself because I'm going mad. I'm no longer able to cope with the pressure. My eyes actually look slightly mad. I try to calm myself down, spray on some perfume, look sadly around me. The evening sun is slanting in the window and faintly, in the distance, I can hear kids on the estate playing and laughing.

I look at myself again. I'm not exactly a beauty but I've no money, gave up work when I got married and he doesn't give me a bob, so I get most of my clothes in second-hand clothes shops – not the fancy designer shops, the mid-range charity shops – and I don't look too bad. Not that I go anywhere now, meet a friend now and then for a coffee, but they're all married with kids, have their own lives; still, I couldn't survive without my friends and the odd cup of coffee. I suppose I should be pragmatic, think about training for a job, but I need to take more urgent action tonight, and then I'll see about doing a back-to-work course. There's a bit of fight in this lady yet.

I know what I've been craving for a long time now – I need to be held, touched, because I'm withering inside. I look around me. The bedroom is small, cluttered, full of junk.

The house we live in is a small semi-detached house in a modest estate. My bed is a jumbled mess and the air smells stale. My clothes are scattered everywhere. I'm neglecting myself, not bothering anymore about my appearance, losing interest. I have forgotten the sensual pleasure of silken underthings, lotions and creams, the pleasure of my body. I awaken in the mornings and curl into a ball of pain where once I used to stretch pleasurably, pull back the curtains and jump from my bed into the shower, coming awake under the cascading water. But that was a long time ago. I had a shower tonight and I started to cry. But I'm willing to do anything to find company tonight, or that last sputtering spark of optimism in me is going to die.

When I married Paul I was so in love, so enraptured by him, so happy. I was introduced to him in a pub and sat down beside him. I was entranced the very moment I met him, entranced by his sweetness. We were married within six months. At the time I was working as a secretary but when he started his business I gave up my job and started to work for him. It was his shy, insecure charm that had won my heart, and the usual spasm of agony passes through me when I think of how loved I felt.

All I want tonight is to be touched, like a dying plant needs water. My vanity is not a player. I do not need to be desired, but I want to hold a man's body, to be held, however briefly, after lovemaking, and I need the visceral release of sex. I want to wrap my arms and legs around a man's body, because something inside me is dying, the very spark of life.

The man downstairs has nearly destroyed me. I had tried so hard to help him when he started drinking, had broken my back trying to put things right, feeling so sorry for him, but he was incapable of ever considering me or anyone else but himself so I suppose I had let him walk all over me, and I am not proud of that. It wasn't really his drinking that finally bothered me — it was his selfishness, and the shameful fact that I had never really considered myself. Now, perhaps, it was too late. Tonight, I knew that I would crawl, like a wounded animal, into anyone's bed.

The hurt was ferocious after he started drinking, the insidious, poisonous abuse, the endless allowances I made for him. I looked at the sad, middle-aged woman in the mirror before me, and I realised that tonight in some curious way I was fighting for my life — my very will to live has been damaged by so much hurt and pain. After he left his job in the civil service and started a business, he had then moved into buying property. He had become such a bully, drinking more and more, and I never knew who was the real man.

Power and influence had somehow driven him insane, and the shy, insecure, sensitive man had completely disappeared to be replaced by a tyrant and a bully. It was as if in over-compensating for an inferiority complex he had begun throwing his weight about, working out some unresolved rage. He had always been careful with money but he became meaner and more grasping as he got richer and richer. When he was sober he leeched onto me emotionally, telling me how bad he felt, drawing the last drop of blood from my body. I did everything I could to help put things right because I so desperately wanted to help him.

My entire life had disappeared, dissolved over the years, had been sucked down the drain. We stopped going out as a couple, stopped going to the theatre or the cinema, and I never went anywhere. I became so lonely. We stopped mixing, nobody invited us to dinner parties anymore and he just spent the nights in the pub, and, no doubt, occasionally picking up some young woman in Leeson Street, impressed because he owned property.

Finally, it had all gone from under him, and he would stagger home from one of his forays into town, his eyes bleary and blood-shot, and collapse across my bed until we had got separate bedrooms. I felt so humiliated, felt so pitied by people, mutual friends who knew he was playing around, that I had gradually reconciled myself to this horror. We never had a child, which would have been some compensation, and I had put aside that longing. And he never became violent. The violence was emotional – the worst kind of violence, the one that completely corrodes. At least after a good beating, there's probably a kiss-and-make-up time, probably some intense emotional bonding that compensates for the pain.

I looked into my eyes again, tried to smile, and the light in my eyes flickered. I used to be able to give that come-hither look but now I haven't a shred of confidence. I wearily applied another layer of mascara and thought about making an appointment with a beautician, but I haven't a bob.

Anyway, a few vodkas would see me right tonight. And drunken, separated men aren't too fussy, nursing their own wounds and battle-scars from failed relationships and broken marriages, probably just looking for a bit of comfort too. I was lonely lying in bed on my own every night.

I wondered had Paul ever loved me, and wondered what was love and was love ever real? There was only one truth – the truth in my own heart, and my heart was in danger because his abuse had finally nearly curdled my blood. He could never consider me, could only ever consider himself and I had simply mistaken weakness for gentleness when I first met him. I had ended up married to a bully and a thug, but I had once truly loved him and knew that the only way to rescue that love was to walk away, to dance. I did a little twirl in front of the mirror and began to hum 'Dancing Queen'. I didn't look that bad. I needed a truly human touch, needed to have my faith in human nature restored. Any drunken half-wit would do. Any inept fumblings, any half-hearted coupling would do. Any yoke hanging around the bar at the end of the night would do, any morsel of humanity. I shuddered slightly, flicked my feather boa over my shoulder and went out into the night. I was anyone's tonight, anyone's at all.

Trudy Hayes has completed an M. Phil in Creative Writing from Trinity College, where she contributed to the anthology *Lemon Soap*, published by the M. Phil class in Creative Writing there. She is currently writing a novel entitled *The Moth-Hour*.

2003

THE PET

Richie Beirne

Richie Beirne was born and bred in Roscommon. He co-wrote the cult radio comedy *Gumgoogly*. He has worked in meat factories, restaurants, convents and as a chef in a montessori school. A racing cyclist fanatic who has even managed to do a stage of the Tour de France, he co-produced the short film *RSVP*. (2003)

He took three sharp breaths. It was dark. All he could hear were the usual night sounds in the field at the back of the house. The twin lights of a car the only relief in the pitch black as it wound its way erratically over the hill. He knew instinctively that it was a neighbour called Maguire trundling home after another night on the town. As the thought flashed by in his head, a dozen images of beer, laughter and sadness ripped through his consciousness and the old familiar ache for them tugged at his heart and body. Then the winter rain started again.

He cursed out loud and spun the torch back and forth in front of him, the beam acting like a sword in front of him, lighting the way. He stopped up short and sniffed deeply. He could almost smell her, the pregnant cow. He lifted out the torch and slowly cast its light in a circle around him. All he could see was the rain and the twin bright unblinking silver eyes of the sheep as they stared back at him. They didn't startle from him like he was a stranger. They recognised these now familiar walks of his late at night. Every two hours, every night, for weeks now. He sighed. The tiredness threatening to overwhelm him. He started to cry but nothing would come. He was all heart-ached out. Then that other ache was back. The ache for warmth, comfort and the blanket — like the woolly numb-ness that alcohol brought as its gift. A temporary respite to his tormented mind. He missed her something terrible. His wife was gone.

One of the sheep bleated and came running to him out of wet gloom and into the light of the torch. It was the pet. His mother had died giving birth to him two months ago and as a result he had to be bottle-fed. The man couldn't close the back door of the house day or night but the pet would hear it almost as if it had special antennae. It always made the man laugh to see the pet scampering over to the house bleating hopefully for more of the good stuff. The man smiled as the lamb came over to him and started savagely butting his head at the man's leg. He tried to pat him on the head as if he was a dog, but the pet just latched onto his hand like it were his mother's teat and began to suck furiously. 'Damn,' said the man as he pulled back his hand sharply. The pet had grown teeth and had cut his fingers with the sucking. The man shone the light on his hand and stared at the bright red blood as it left his fingers and started to flow down his hand in little rivers. But the pet wasn't going to stop and continued to scurry around him, thrusting his head up under the green wax jacket, biting and sucking, looking for the teat that was never there.

The man shook himself violently, as if to remind himself of what he was about. 'No point dwelling on it now, get on with it,' he said to himself as he gave the pet a quick kick to the stomach and strode purposefully forward into the dark. The pet let a grunt out of him and stayed where he was. The lamb knew the routine by now. There was no sweet milk coming from the man tonight – well at least not this time – and so the pet turned around and strayed back to the flock. The man stopped up short and shone the light back at the pet, already sorry for the kick, and watched as the pet also stopped waiting in the solitary light of the torch to see if there was a hope. But there was none so the lamb shook his rain sodden head and settled down at the edge of the flock where no one wanted him, on the edges, marginalised. That made the man sad again. With that the ache got stronger as the pain washed in. The craving for alcohol opened up in him as if it sensed a weakness, an opening. It was like a parasite, feeding off him, pouncing on him, never letting him go.

She had left him two weeks ago and the memory electrocuted his heart. He stared up at the black sky. His face stretched back, baring it to the rain. He opened his mouth wide; his tongue stuck out obscenely as he tried to express what he couldn't. All that came out was a low whine like a dog being beaten. He breathed out and walked on, his shoulders slumped, the ground turning to mud under his feet as he walked the endless patrol of the night. Every night now he was up. There was no relief. No help. He was on his own now, tending the farm. He was as thin as a rake. His trilby hat flopped on his head as the rain weighted it down. He hadn't eaten in two days. He knew it was bad, but there was no room in him for anything else. He was full of emptiness. But the stock needed him. They depended on him, especially in such bad weather. Only for him they would starve in the winter. Their dependence had kept him going these last two weeks. He would have gone out of his mind otherwise. Then the man started to laugh, sure maybe he was already mad. He hadn't seen anyone in the two weeks since she had walked out. The closest contact he'd had to people were the cars at night making their way home in the distance. He started to cry again. This time a few tears came. He was almost relieved that there was something left inside him.

'Where was the bloody bitch,' he growled at the night. He shook himself again, an old habit, and strode forward strongly. Each step a walking away from the dead thing he left behind. His back was straighter and there was almost a jaunt in his step. He waved the torch in front of him like a scythe, cutting through the darkness and the rain. Nothing. He started to fret. The cow was due to calve three weeks ago and it was getting serious. The calf would be a big one and he knew it would be a hard birth. It was the cow's first calving and she was nervous and agitated. She roamed the small back field day and night. She had worn a rough wet track around the edges of the field, seeking peace from these new instincts that tormented her flesh and her dulled mind. The man needed the calf. It wasn't for the money, mind, although that was needed too. There just didn't seem to be much else left to live for. He wanted the calf to live desperately; it had become a mission for him, to see the yet unborn calf live. He stopped up short. There was a sound. He sniffed deeply and smelled her again. She was near calving. He knew it. He could smell it. He hurried towards the sound and there she was stretched out like a beached whale on the wet ground under the hawthorn bush. She had decided that this was the place and had given herself up.

The calf wouldn't wait anymore. The man slowed down and turned off the torch. He didn't want to frighten her or she'd take off around the field. That would be a disaster. He smiled grimly. His whole body tensed, making small unintelligible sounds to comfort the worried beast. He stepped carefully towards her as if on ice.

The cow spotted him and raised her head wearily and moaned. 'It's alright girl, easy now easy now, shhh, that's the girl, good girl,' he whispered. She threw her head back and lowed out loud, relieved and scared at the same time. The man was excited now and his instincts took over. He was happy now, familiar with this. He had done it a thousand times before. He had a talent for this. It was what he knew. He felt safe and anxious all at the same time. On a knife edge of hope and death. The calf was half-way out of the cow but was stuck at the hips. He expected this as he knew the calf would be too big. The rain started to ease off and for that he was glad, a little help at last perhaps. The cow strained her head, her eyes wide open with pain as she strove to expel this body from her. She was terrified. The ground was all wet and churned up where she had worried herself around and around, picking her spot. The man turned on the torch again and laid it on the ground, pointing the light at the cow's behind where the half born calf shook and spluttered trying to break free. The man lost all hesitation now. The cow wasn't going to get up and go now: she was too far gone in her pain and fear. He grabbed the calf's head, which was slimy with mucus, and stuck his bloodied hand into its mouth to see if it'd suck. It did. It was alive! There was hope. He scooped out the mucus from the calf's mouth so that it wouldn't choke. It was a bull calf. He knew by the size of it. 'Brilliant, worth a fortune,' he smiled to himself, a bit of luck at last maybe. The man settled onto his knees and started to sink in the muck. He took out two pieces of rope from his pockets that he always had close to hand for just such an emergency like this and slipped the ready made loops onto the calf's feet. He tightened the hangman's noose on each foot just above the joint where it would get a grip and planted his two feet either side of the half born calf and onto the cow's behind. He wound the ropes tightly around his hands and braced himself, waiting for the cow to give the next heave. You can't force it. It was always better to work with the animal. The phrases came to his mind easily as he remembered what he had learnt from his own father and had hoped one day to pass onto his own son. But not now, that was all gone. 'Oh, Jesus wept,' he cried as another sharp pain of loss cut through him. Then the cow started to push and the man pulled with her. She stopped and he stopped, checking to see if the calf was alright, all the while talking quietly to the cow, reassuring her, encouraging her, willing her to push harder. They were one now: the cow, the calf and the man alone in the middle of the night. Each desperately trying to live. To survive, to breathe, to exist. The man was pulling with all his might, his whole body taut with the pressure. The rope was cutting into his hands, his face an expression of extreme. His hat fell off as he slid in the muck and the ropes went slack. The cow was having trouble. 'The calf won't last long at this rate,' the man thought. 'Shit,' he said. The man knelt close to the calf's head and watched as the calf sputtered and choked, shaking its head weakly with the effort. The man braced himself again and pulled but no give. He sensed the cow was getting tired and he knew she was starting to give up. It was a matter of seconds now, he knew. He was worried. He got ready again and began to pull but no joy. The calf was dying now. 'Fuck,' he cursed and got ready to pull again.

The calf was simply too big and the man wasn't strong enough to pull him free. He sat back for a minute, staring at the calf breathing shallowly, and then he started to get mad. There was no way on this wide earthly world this calf was going to die. He grimly set his feet down again and grabbed the two soaking wet ropes and began to pull with ferocious rage. The anger gave him strength. Anger at her leaving him. Anger at his miserable life and anger mostly at himself. He cursed and roared and yelled as he pulled. The cow also started bellowing, surprised at this new sudden onslaught of pain. The calf tried to utter some sound but was fading fast. 'Don't die on me yet, don't die on me yet, you bastard,' and the man pulled even tighter. He was stretched out tight at the back of the cow. Leaning into the pull, using his weight and momentum to force the calf out. He roared again, but this time at the cow to push and push she did. There was a second when he thought he was going to have a heart attack, when out burst the calf and the man catapulted back on the ground and landed on his own backside in the muck and wet grass. The shock of the sudden act dazed him for a second or two but then he crawled forward, begging and hoping in the name of God that the calf was alive. 'Please God, Please God let him live,' he pleaded.

The calf was dead. It had been too long hanging out and it was too weak with all the rain and the cold and the effort of trying to get out. The cow raised herself up on her feet and was trying to lick the calf clean of the afterbirth and was as yet unsure why her calf wasn't trying to get up on its feet. The man knelt in the muck beside the calf. The rain started to pour down once again. He felt he wasn't there anymore, that he was watching himself collapse and melt away with the rain in front of his own eyes. He started to shake and cry. Great heaving sobs that wracked his frail and battered body. He cried his wife's name over and over again, just saying her name as he wrapped his arms around himself and rocked back and forth, back and forth. Hopeless, desolate and beyond help. The ropes were still wound around his hands, tightly bound, and his hands were going blue. The man looked at the ropes, the dead calf, and spat out the rain, tears and snot that were falling into his mouth. He stared up at the hawthorn bush and not for the first time thought about an end to all this pain. He started to loosen the noose around the dead calf's leg and slipped it free. He stared at the noose, the idea growing stronger in his mind. The more he thought about it the more the pain and aches started to wash away. He started to cry again and turned his head away from the sight of the calf and its confused mother and began to rise when he felt something hitting him in the back. For a brief bright moment he thought that the calf had somehow started to kick and breathe. But when he looked around it was the pet lamb again nudging him and trying to suck the corner of his coat. He stared down dumbly at the lamb sucking frantically as the rain teemed down around them in the middle of the night.

Richie Beirne is currently working with RTÉ Radio One.

HAWK

Breda Wall Ryan

Breda Wall Ryan is a native of Waterford,
was educated at UCC and now works as a
teacher of English as a foreign language in
Bray, where she lives with her family. She is
attending Dermot Bolger's masterclasses at
TCD. This is her first published fiction.
(2003)

It is September and the children
have returned to school after the
long summer holiday. I am walking
in the foothills of the Comeraghs towards the lake that is a legacy of the
ice age and the grim cliffs that have
backed the lake since a glacier gouged
out the corrie from the basalt. I am
glad that I am alone and free from
the bickering of my children who
have squandered a week jostling for
position within the family. I wish
they were little again and filled with
wonder, or else older so that I might
topple them from the nest. Then I
feel the wish is unworthy and I push

it aside, and am sorry I did not leave them a note to say
where I have gone.

I turn aside from the path that leads to the cold blackness
of the lake and the precipice that is always slick with the run-
off from the mountain. On that cliff-face a pair of peregrine
falcons scraped off a ledge and hatched a clutch in each of
the last four years. I hear the scream of a falcon now, but I
cannot find him in the blue vastness above the rockface. My
roots are here; it was my grandmother's home.

I trace the outline of the farmhouse. When the thatch
gave way, rain soaked into the cob, the walls folded in on
themselves. Part of the wide stone chimney still stands. A
rope of ivy thick as a man's thigh gropes upwards from the
base, dark with glossy leaves.

A box hedge climbs to fifteen feet, its base bare from the
depredations of sheep. The escallonia, left unchecked, fills
the haggard. The hedge behind the bones of a farmyard
drips fuchsia, the flowers like purple-skirted ballerinas, each
with a drop of nectar in her belly. I think of my grandmother's nine brothers, and how the farm was too small, the
soil too sparse to support more than one.

'Only good for growing rocks,' my grandmother used to
say. She took a slip of the pink climbing rose with the
blooms like wadded tissue with her when she married my
grandfather with his broad acres of riverside land. But her
roots lay deep here and a yearning for the mountain farm
tugged against the contrary pull of her new home. It was to
the Comeraghs she looked for her weather forecast.

'*Caipín ar Chruachán agus Coum Siongán ag caitheamh tabac. Tá
an fearthainn ag teacht.*' Then the rain would surely fall. And it
was to the heart-rending laments of the Comeraghs she
turned to sing herself out of her yearning, 'Sliabh Gua' or
'Priosún Cluain Meala'.

'My eight brothers scattered through the streets of New
York or were swallowed up in the Welsh mines. Two were

crushed under the weight of falling coal, and the weight of loneliness crushed the youngest two. It's an unnatural place, a mine, under the mountain.' And my grandmother would sigh then and say that her eldest brother never married and the mountain reclaimed the land that her ancestors had wrested from it.

I think I will collect some fuchsia and suck the nectar from it and that it will be as sweet now as it is in memory. I push past the tangle of *buachallán buí* and *neantóg* and *capóg* and scutchgrass and I note the soft hollow sound my boot makes when it meets a rotten plank of wood. I realise that there is a covered well here at the back of the ruined farm-house even as I am falling through. I hear a sharp snap like the crack of a dry branch snapped by a footstep and pain like no pain I have ever felt before rips through my leg.

'My leg, my leg!' I wail and then I sob like a little child because there is no one to hear me. A thick welt rises across my shin and then the flesh covering the break begins to swell until the leg is twice the size of its partner and the skin is taut and shiny and I think it might burst. I am glad that I am wearing wide-legged trousers that will not need to be torn away from the damaged limb. I am surprised that I can think about such things and at the same time weep because of the pain that is now like a knife through the long bones from my heel to my knee. Fat tears slide separately down my cheeks and run together under my chin and I wipe with the back of my wrist at the snail-trails they must leave on my face. I think that when the pain subsides or when I grow used to it, I will try to climb out of this hole. The fall was not long, no more than a second I think, but when I look up the surface of the earth is twenty feet above me and the sky above that seems very close. I hear the falcon scream, and I know he has killed and will be tearing the throat from a thrush or a rabbit and devouring the still-bleeding flesh.

I call for help for a long time but then my voice grows

thin and I stop. I must save it for when someone comes near. I regret tucking the car out of sight behind the stand of spruce. I had thought to avoid vandalism. Now I realise I should have left the car in full view, so the ranger would search when I failed to return. I look up when I hear the falcon again, but I see only the contrail of a jet unzipping the sky.

All day I hear the falcon scream while he quarters his hunting ground. I am in a chimney built of rough-cut stone with a cobbled floor. When I shout, my voice echoes and I do not know if the waves of sound arrive at the surface, or arrive there only as whispers. The falcon's shriek penetrates to the depths of the well. Its pitch is high and clear and it trails no echo.

My leg throbs and I am so cold now that I have stopped shivering. I know I should cover my head to prevent the loss of precious body heat. Instead, I take off my fleece jacket and wrap it around my feet. My feet are freezing and I need to keep the circulation going but I can move only the left one.

My right foot, on the leg that is broken, looks black. When I touch it with a fingertip, a touch light as a butterfly, a scalding sensation spreads across the skin. I think about gangrene and then I decide not to think about that at all, and I think of the peregrines soaring on an updraft and of the photographs Dan took of them last month.

On the slimy floor of the well are maybe two inches of water, and I sit in this water since I have no other option. There is no ledge onto which I might drag myself, and besides I think I might do more damage to my leg or pass out from the pain. I remember hearing of someone drowning in two inches of rainwater after falling into an emptied swimming pool, and I do not want to drown. This is not a fresh-spring well. It is a kind of cistern fed by a rivulet. The overflow lies above my head and is lined with stone in the manner of a French drain. If I am careful not to pass out I will not drown, since we have had two weeks without rain. But if the weather changes it will be a different story.

The late sun is flushing pink across the hole in the roof of the well and I decide I will not think about the worst possible scenario until it happens. The falcon screams again. Something plummets straight down and lands with the muffled sound of a bag of flour dropped on a kitchen floor, absorbing its own impact. It is followed by the sound of a single shot, so closely that one seems a grace note of the other. At first I think that the feathered sack on the well floor is lifeless. Then I think of the gunman and I scream for help. Surely he will search for his kill to make sure of its death and finish it off if need be? But the sky greys with the coming of night and no rescue comes. Then I am filled with despair. I think of my granduncles who slipped their necks through a noose rather than spend another night or day underground. And I feel a great pity for them.

I stare at the creature lying on the well floor opposite me. The feathers of his back are bluish grey in the twilight, and his underparts are a dirty yellow-white with black barring, and I think this peregrine will not hunt again. I reach out to touch the poor broken creature. Then I notice the faint rapid flicker in his breast and I pull my hand back. One of his wings trails in the dregs of the well, like a broken umbrella abandoned in a storm. I wonder if I should despatch him with a rock and end his suffering, but the only loose rock on the floor of the well is too heavy. I think that even if I could stand, and my leg was not broken, I could not summon the courage to stamp on the bird's head and finish the gunman's work. The falcon's head is sideways on to me, and as I think about a mercy killing, the falcon's eye opens and he fixes me with his stare. The inner membrane of his eye flickers like a camera shutter across the eyeball, and the bird raises first his speckled head with the vicious curved beak, and then his body, so that he is sitting low like a broody hen in the murky water. He keeps me in his sights while he gathers strength to his body. I hold his gaze, afraid to blink because now the creature I felt such pity for appears to me malevolent. He fixes me with his fish-eye and we each lie perfectly still in our own section of the circular stone tomb.

'I know you're hurt, and you do not know what to do for the pain, but in the morning they'll come to find me and then they'll save you, too,' I soothe the wounded bird. But I hear fear in my voice, and fall silent.

I am beyond cold now. I can no longer feel my feet. The thirst I felt before twilight is gone. The desire to sleep over-whelms me.

Even as I fight exhaustion, the falcon gains strength. He shakes his head and fluffs his ruffs of plumage to insulate his body. His watchfulness increases and I force myself to stay awake though my eyelids are gritty with sleep.

The moon is a night away from full. A beam strikes the rim of the well. It fingers its way down the stone shaft, pull-ing the cold white lamp higher in the night sky until it lies directly overhead. The falcon's refracting eyes glitter. His stare does not falter. He stands up now in the moonlight and I see he is at least eighteen inches from hooked beak to tail feathers. He spreads his good wing and hops to catch an updraft, but when he fails to get airborne he gives up and clings to the tumbled rock with his talons.

'He has gained the high ground,' I think and I wonder why at first I had felt sorry for him. He is a predator and a predator does not show mercy. An image from a horror film flashes into my mind, of a tortured captive whose eyes have been gouged out with an iron spike. I do not want to dwell on such an image, and I push the memory aside.

The falcon spreads his wings. The broken wing has no voluntary movement, but the good wing opens like a fan, and he rattles it as a Spanish dancer rattles the tortoiseshell ribs of her *abanico*. He is displaying his superiority, I think, and I try to haul myself into a more upright position because I know that the way I am slumped marks me as a victim.

Then another image forms, this one from my childhood, of a pair of young rams tangled in a thicket. Something startled them so that they ran for cover, and their thrashing to break free tightened the whips of brambles in their fleeces. They were held fast, and the scald-crows swooped and perched on their heads and employed their coal-pick beaks to peck out their eyes. They gorged on the eyeballs and they penetrated to the brain and feasted on that, too. My father despatched me to fetch his gun and a box of bullets and he put the beasts out of their misery. And over the following weeks and months he shot every scald-crow he got in his sights and hung their stinking carcasses from the rowans around the headlands of the fields.

I think about the falcon again now, how someone has shot him because he killed, maybe, a pet or a farmyard fowl. His instinct is to kill, and he is strong again now in spite of the broken wing. I am weak from pain and cold and I believe that my desire to sleep is the onset of hypothermia. And I know I should remain motionless because a peregrine detects the slightest movement from a great distance, and drops like a stone to strike with clenched talons and kill by impact. This falcon cannot gain the height he needs for a strike, but if I sleep or pass out I think he will tear at the orbs of my eyes and scoop out the soft grey-pink porridge that lies within the outer membrane of my brain.

I push that image down and watch the falcon whose eyes are fixed on my face and do not waver. His plumage has lost its sheen, but the peregrine is still very beautiful and I am sorry for him because we are each of us broken. But he is still a predator and without pity and he watches for the least movement. The living death of the lambs under their crown of scald-crows flashes back into my mind and instinct raises my hands to cover my eyes.

Since 'Hawk' appeared in New Irish Writing, Breda Wall Ryan has read for an M. Phil. in Creative Writing at Trinity College. Her stories have appeared in the anthology *Moments* and she was among the writers short-listed for the Davy Byrne Award. A novel is close to completion and she is also working on a collection of short fiction.

WHERE SHE
BELONGS

Noëlle Harrison

Noëlle Harrison lives in Oldcastle, Co.
Meath, and currently works as a resource
teacher and part-time lecturer in Art History. She has written two stage plays which
were performed in Dublin. In 1997 she won
the Bookwise Short Story Competition and
she was short-listed for the Molly Keane
Award in 2002. Since submitting *Where She
Belongs*, which is her first published fiction,
she has been taken on by the literary agent
Marianne Gunn O'Connor and has just
signed a two book deal with Pan Macmillan
and Tivoli. Her first novel, *Beatrice*, is due to
be published in August 2004. (2003)

Had she imagined it or did they
really make love under the Aspen
trees? Yes, they had. It was coming
back to her now. They had followed
his father's trail to the bog, but he had
pulled her aside then, pointed to the
cluster of trees and whispered how he
had always dreamed of making love
there. It had surprised her. He had

never made the first moves. So she followed him, more curious than excited.

She remembered that there were a cluster of young Aspens, slender, gentle and chiding them in the breeze. Below the grass grew tall, in patches flattened by strong winds the night before. Beside them the land slid into a ditch, a trickle of brown bog water passing them by. She could recall nothing else, except there was a donkey, an indifferent witness to what they did, and the scent of the land around upon which she lay. She would never forget that. That was what had attracted her to him in the first place.

They both lived in Dublin. But their relationship existed here, in the country. Every Friday night, at exactly six o'clock, he collected her on his Honda Four Fifty. At first they would be setting off in daylight, arriving just as the sun was going down. Now it was dark when they left, and each week getting colder. He had given her a leather jacket someone had left behind in his house in Dublin, and told her to stuff newspapers inside it to keep her warm. As well as this she was wearing a thick sweater, a pair of leggings, jeans, waterproof trousers and three pairs of socks. Still her kidneys ached.

They exchanged few words, but on the bike, they melded. It was all down to gesture, touch, intuition. Her arms were wrapped around his waist, the velocity of the machine pushing her into his back. She was so incredibly attracted to his control over the motorbike, to the necessity of his minding her. Sometimes when they stopped at traffic lights, he would pat her knee. She loved this, it was so simple; it was like something your father would do.

Like clockwork they always stopped in Virginia. He would have a mug of tea, and she had coffee, white, scalding hot with a huge blob of cream floating in it. Not long after this, their journey would take them off the main roads, and they would be spinning along in the creeping night, further into the interior, following tiny arteries of lanes, until the final ascent up a pot-holed, overgrown boreen. Before they went into the house, always they stood looking at the lake, a slice of silver, blocked in parts by the silhouettes of tall, evergreen trees. Sometimes he held her hand, his bike helmet in the other, sniffing the air. She could feel five days of city shedding away, a point in her spine, pulling her down, backwards, towards the ground as if an invisible thread held her there. She was invaded by the deep, pungent smell of earth, aeons of mulch, overcoming her, blocking out all desire for moving forwards or back.

In the city it was different. She was always on the lookout for something new. Unable to hold down a job for longer than four weeks, unable to settle in any fixed place, only there two months, stepping off the plane with a striped laundry bag stuffed with clothes, and already looking for somewhere new, her bedroom littered with *Rough Guides* and *Lonely Planets*. Now here she was, standing in front of his homestead, in the utter still of late October, leaves spinning down, everything rewound to slow motion. In his belonging, she could belong.

The first time they came down, his father had taken them to see the horses. It was still warm then, and she followed the men as they had taken off across the fields, the grass gone to meadow and her skin prickling with heat. She had sat on a fence and watched her boyfriend as he had leapt onto a pony, gripped it by the mane and begun to canter around. His father came towards her, speaking fast.

'Go on wit' ye, an' be getting up on this one so.'

She shook her head, she couldn't understand what he was saying, but he was indicating the second pony, the mane of which he had grasped in his hand. It was bareback and skittish.

'No, no thank you.'

'Ah go on wit' ye, are ye afeard?' his father laughed, his broad head encircled by a swarm of gnats.

She gripped the fence, shaking her head, flicking away the flies. Her boyfriend rode towards her.

'Will you not try it?' he asked.

'No, really, I don't want to.'

She saw the disappointment in his eyes. She was a coward.

It was a season of rainbows. That's what she thought to herself. As they spun along the country lanes, intermittently showered on and dried by the last ebb of late autumnal sun.

He spoke about his childhood. There were nine born, five boys and four girls. One of the boys had died at birth. Since that time none of the family went to Mass. Not since the day the priest refused to bury the unbaptised child. All this was strange to her. Four boys sleeping in one room, the four girls in the other, while the parents slept in what looked like an airing cupboard. Every morning his mother made porridge. He could not abide it now. She thought about them all crammed into that tiny cottage by the lake. Then she thought about her own childhood and all she could see were big empty rooms, polished floors and the noise of traffic outside.

He said that sometimes he'd slept in the barn with the cattle, just to have a place of his own, with his head upon a cow's neck. She had shuddered. 'Couldn't that be dangerous? Wasn't it smelly?' 'No,' he smiled, 'it was nice, really safe.'

When they sat at the kitchen table with his mam, as she poured the tea, she imagined the eight children all running around. Now they were all gone – to England or America. Her boyfriend was a homebird. He hated the city, he said, he couldn't wait to be finished up there, and come back home and settle down, and have a family of his own. She said nothing. They both knew it wouldn't be with her.

Sometimes when she stayed in the cottage, she dreamed poems, woke up with the words tripping out of her mind.

Scrambling out of the bed she'd try to write them down, but they were gone. It was like trying to catch sunlight in a jar.

He slept in the boys' room, and she slept in the girls'. Some weekends he would come into her, and lie down next to her, pull back the curtains, and holding her in his arms, look at the stars. Then he would slowly trace her body with his fingertips, not touching but just hovering over her skin, roaming each tiny corner of her. He was in no hurry. The delicacy of these gestures stunned her.

In Dublin it was different. Occasionally she would turn up at his place, which he shared with two other bikers, in a run-down housing estate. She became a dominatrix — making him go to bed early, switching out the light and going down on him. He did not like it, not one little bit.

Once she went to a bike rally with him. As soon as they arrived, as he was surrounded by his mates in leather and their pillion girls in tight T-shirts and jeans, she realised it was a mistake. She sat all day by the tent, getting stoned and watching the men race up and down, doing silly competitions on their bikes, as the girls alternatively eyed her and ignored her. That night there was a band and disco in the pub. She drank as much as she could, but still she was unable to relax. She watched her boyfriend now, drinking beer, laughing at sexist jokes and burping with the rest. Then she was afraid because she did not belong. And her longing was to go now, far, fast, far, far away.

They had met during the summer. She was staying with a friend in the country, when he called by to deliver logs. She had been swimming in the lake and was sitting on a rock outside Gill's back door rolling a joint. Her hair was long, wild, curly and wet, leaking tiny streams of water down her back. She was wearing just an old pair of denim dungarees and bare feet, still brown, from her recent trip to Spain, still feeling abroad. He sat down and smoked with her, then asked her if she needed a ride back to Dublin. He had a motorbike. She loved bikes.

As September ran to October, and then November came along, she stopped going to his house in Dublin altogether. She did not call him during the week, nor he her. They existed for Friday night, Saturday, Sunday – secret weekends, within which to hide, to keep her going for another week.

He knew every tree, each plant, every single flower on his land. She couldn't even remember what they had grown in the window box on her bedroom sill. The one her father had given her before he left.

In London every season had nearly been the same. Here they built bonfires, stacked with dead leaves. She couldn't shake this from her now; woodsmoke always meant winter coming, the beginning of the end.

Then one weekend she could not go. Her period was due on the Monday but it did not come. By Thursday she knew she was pregnant. By Friday she had her ticket booked and flew that evening. As the plane took off from Dublin airport, she could see the housing estates nearby, their blinking orange streetlights, and she imagined him now setting off, making his way across the city and to her front door, and standing there, waiting for her to come down. How long would he stand there she wondered? How long would he wait? As long as it took him to trace her body at night? As long as it took the moon to rise over his homestead lake? She closed her eyes and tried to banish him from her thoughts. But she could see his figure, in black leather, on his bike, riding across her eyeballs, down those little lanes, on and on, riding away from her.

The next week she waited for him. In London she had bought a pair of leather trousers and cut her hair. She had made her eyes cat's eyes with black kohl and painted her lips red. She waited all night. The meter ran out, and she sat in the dark, the scent of her lipstick making her feel sick. Finally she drifted off, and woke with a start. Tired and frightened, a grey Dublin dawn filtered through; she could hear cars starting up, a bus swishing by, as it lashed outside. She curled up in a ball, her hope fading in the growing daylight.

She only saw him twice after that. The following summer, her friend Gill got married, and he was there at the wedding. He had a new girlfriend, one of the pillion girls, and he had his arm round her waist, as she showed off her engagement ring. When the girl disappeared to the toilet, she didn't think twice, she just walked right over to him.

'Would you like to dance?' she asked him.

'Your hair's different,' he said.

'Would you like to dance?' she asked again.

'No,' he said

'Come on, please,' she begged.

'I said I didn't want to,' he said coldly.

'Well fuck you!' she hissed, and walked off to the bar.

Later, much later, he followed her outside. It was nearly dawn, and the party was almost over.

'Are you alright?' he asked.

'Fuck you!' She was drunk.

'Jesus, it was you who stood me up ...'

He scratched his head, looked like a boy.

'Why didn't you call me?' she whined softly.

'Well ... why didn't you phone me? It was you who broke it up ...'

She said nothing. What was the point anymore?

'Listen, do you want to go for a ride?'

He touched her arm, gently, and she looked at him, surprised.

'On the bike ...' he added, smiling.

'What about your girlfriend?'

'She's gone to bed. Come on.'

He handed her the helmet – the same old one. And she followed him down the steps. They took off. It was five o'clock in the morning, late May, and already the sun was coming out. She opened her mouth and tasted the bite in the day, the mist burning off. They sped along, as tiny birds swooped around them, darting in between their bodies. They dived straight down out of the sky, kamikaze style. Around her the air was humming, thick with their tiny propelled bodies, their frenzied wings. He pulled over and took off his helmet.

'We'd better wait,' he said. 'It's dangerous.'

'Oh my God!' she said. 'The noise!'

They stood together, watching the cacophony. Then he turned to her.

'Where *were* you that day?' he sounded desperate.

'I was in London,' she replied.

'Gill told me you were alright. I did ring her, I was worried ... but when she said you were fine, I just figured you'd had enough.'

'Enough of what?'

'Of me. I'm not an *eejit* you know. I'd sussed you weren't sticking around. Can't believe you're still here; I thought you would have moved on by now.'

'Yeah, well, I'm not gone yet.'

'Why didn't you tell me you were going to London? Why was it such a big secret?'

'I couldn't ... I had to go suddenly ... Well, there's only one reason to go to London fast, and in secret,' she spat out.

He stared at her, long, hard. He understood now what she meant. His eyes filled up with disgust. He knew it; she was a coward.

'You could have told me!' he choked, and then putting on his helmet he cut off all other communication.

'I ... I wanted to,' she said, looking at herself in his visor. 'But I didn't belong. I didn't want to marry you – you would have wanted that – wouldn't you? Wouldn't you?'

He turned on the ignition, revved the bike. Obediently she got on the back. He turned it and made towards the hotel. She twisted her arms behind her and held onto the back of the bike, not wanting to touch him. He picked up speed. The wind cut into her, birds crashed around her and she could feel herself being pushed back. It would be so easy, just to let go now; she felt removed from her body, suspended by speed in mid-air. Faster they went, taking off over hump-backs, screeching round bends: he was trying to frighten her now. She could see his eyes in the wing mirror; he was switched off to her. He propelled them forwards. Vaguely she wondered how much he had drunk – he was doing a ton at least. Then, just as suddenly, he braked, her hands lost their grip and she slammed into his back. He pushed her leg back. The same hand that had patted her knee now repelled her. She stumbled off the bike, dropping the helmet and running into the hotel.

The last time she saw him was five years later. He turned up on her doorstep one day. She had just put the baby down for a sleep when the knock came. Seeing him there, with shorter hair and browner skin, knocked her back. He said that Gill had given him the address, and that he had been away for several years, in Australia. He was back now for a short time, but heading off again shortly for Africa.

She brought him in and made tea. Shy for a few minutes, it was she who spoke first.

'What about that girl? Did you not get married?' she asked.

'No, I broke it off, soon after. She was cheating on me.'

'Oh, I'm sorry,' she said.

They sat in silence for a while. Then he just looked at her, not quite believing what he was taking in.

'Look at you,' he said quietly, spreading his arms, 'just look at how beautiful you are.'

She blushed. 'Hardly. I'm six months pregnant.'

He shook his head.

'Here you are,' he said, 'where I belong. You have it now see – in the country, in a cottage with your husband, and your child. It's rich, is it not?'

He stood and took her hand. He lifted it to his nostrils and smelt her skin; he closed his eyes and remembered the Aspen trees.

'I'm sorry,' she said. 'So sorry ...'

'So am I ...'

He left as she fed her baby. He looked back once, half-way down the lane. She stood at the open doorway of her home, and he saw her take the baby's tiny head and lift it to her breast, saw it latch on and suck. Then he faced away again and kept on walking.

The sun dipped down in front of him and turned his figure black, and it occurred to her why she had chosen this life. By marrying her husband, by living in this place, by having two babies, she had tried to resurrect what he had been to her. She remembered everything now; each tiny detail under the Aspen trees, when he had made love to her, and as the swaying trees played tricks with the light, fragmenting each moment, dappling her senses, she remembered that second in which they eclipsed, in which she conceived.

Noëlle Harrison's debut novel *Beatrice* was published in 2004 by Tivoli/Pan Macmillan to considerable critical acclaim. A new play, *The Good Sister*, has since been premiered in The Ramor Theatre, Cavan, and her second novel, *A Small Part of Me*, was published by Tivoli/Pan Macmillan in September 2005.

2004

OSTRICH

Eileen Brannigan

Eileen Brannigan was born in Belfast and grew up between there and the family farm in Co. Monaghan, moving later to Dublin to attend TCD. Since then she has worked in publishing, human rights and arts education, with bouts of creative endeavour in between. She currently lives in Co. Donegal. This is her first published work. (2004)

Ostriches, Struthio camelus, *are the largest living bird in the world. They are flightless but are fast runners. Contrary to popular belief, ostriches do not bury their heads in the sand.*

All movement had suddenly stopped. The engine noise had ceased. The Ostrich ruffled its stiffened feathers and peered through the slats in the tall crate. Nothing but darkness. The air was dank. Sudden rattle, a chink of light and with it a gust of air, ammonia laden. Smelled like dung. And for an instant all was familiar again. For an instant the sun blazed fiercely above a lone plane tree, jagged sculpture in a vast terracotta flatland. Rumbling swirls of orange dust, distant dazzle of zebra. Giraffes gliding dreamlike across the grassland. A shiny black beetle crossing the fissures in the baked red earth, zealously rolling a ball of elephant dung, musky and sweet smelling. The beetle rolls its mammoth parcel past an unimpressed lizard basking on a stone, flicking its sticky tongue. Past a sleeping snake, coils glistening in the sun. Past a dome of enormous white eggs, one beginning to crack. The dung beetle halts momentarily to reposition itself, get a better hold on its burden. The crack in the eggshell splits. A tiny beak emerges. Scaldy head on tenuous, drunken neck. Claggy with yolk sac, the newborn pecks haphazardly at the dust, captures the resting beetle in its beak. Consumes the writhing mouthful greedily. The young bird swallows, shakes its scraggy head, surveys the immense plains all around it with unblinking yellow eyes.

Clattering, rattling, raised voices, scringing of hinges. A square of watery, grey light. Unfamiliar. Silhouetted in the doorway, men in caps, with sticks.

Adult ostriches usually weigh between 150 to 330 pounds and stand up to 9 feet tall.

'Christ above, Ignatius. That's a desperate lookin' yoke.'

Larry stared at the Ostrich, bedraggled in the rain. The Ostrich stared back at the man in the tattered cap with the flat, sceptical face and jutting ears. 'That's some divil to have lookin' at ye over yer own hedge.' Larry shook his bony head, spat derisively through ill spaced teeth.

'It's not their looks I'm buying them for.' Ignatius winked. He lowered his voice confidentially. Larry leaned in.

'You can get two grand and over for a young bird. Up to ten times as much for a good breeding bird. And the female will lay ...' he paused for effect '... up to *eighty* eggs in a season. I may have only two pair now but ... you do the sums yourself.'

Larry whistled, his watery eyes narrowing, surveying the bird with renewed interest.

'Money burning a hole in your pocket. Guaranteed. No more TB, no more BSE. I'm telling you, Larry. Beef has had its day. This here is the future of farming.' Ignatius pointed his pipe confidently at the scaldy looking bird before them.

In the months before, Ignatius had been having a recurring vision of himself. Increasingly it had floated without warning into his waking thoughts as often as his sleeping. He saw himself as a haggard old man, bowed with rheumatism, shuffling an ever-dwindling herd of cattle endlessly from one field to another, until that final field with the tombstone in it. And he knew what name was upon the tilted stone. His cattle nosing around the sweet grasses at its foot, as if he had never existed. And he had awoken one cold morning, sweating, heart hammering in his throat, and resolved to do something about it.

Down in the pub that Saturday evening Ignatius was greeted with special interest and attention; slapped on the back by some, jibed good-naturedly by the others. He reacted with pink-faced pride, like an expectant father. And whatever about the jokes, he found he hardly had to put his hand in his pocket the whole night. When he staggered back in the early hours, the craic and banter still ringing in his ears, he went to inspect his stock.

In the moonlight, they appeared like grey ghosts, huge eyes reflecting the planets. Alien. Even with the few drinks in him, they were unnerving in their nighttime strangeness, their profound otherness. And a small shiver of doubt goosed his whiskey-warmed skin. He felt them watch him silently as he went back into the house.

The following morning, despite his hangover, Ignatius had a hen egg for his breakfast. And as he tapped the shell with his spoon he thought with satisfaction that it would take two dozen of these to make up one single ostrich egg.

March was approaching and Ignatius looked for signs that his birds were coming into season. The days passed. Each morning he looked hopefully in the shed. But each morning he would find the birds simply standing in a huddle out of the drizzle, eyeing him with remote curiosity.

The days turned into weeks. And the weeks passed. And still not one single, solitary egg. Not even the sign of a nest dug into the dirt. He scoured his breeders' journals and books forensically.

Breeding season length largely depends on food availability, bird condition and weather. Bird condition is important as unhealthy and improperly conditioned birds will often be less productive egg layers.

With increasing anxiety, Ignatius began to check and re-check everything. He changed the feed to the best quality ratite he could buy. He raked the sand in the rolling pit, laid fresh bedding on the shed floor every day, repaired the tiniest gaps in the shed walls where draughts might be getting through. And after finally ruling out everything else, he began to look to the skies, which were slate grey and ominously swollen.

March turned into April, which became May. Rain flooded the paddocks and the alfalfa seed that he had planted as forage failed to thrive. In June he started buying in alfalfa pellets instead. He had to order them from England and they were expensive. He watched for moulting or any signs of illness in the birds but he could spot nothing physically wrong. He was careful to examine the birds only when they were securely confined, because they had taken to running at him, wings extended, in a most aggressive way.

Handling ostriches can be dangerous to the bird and handler. A mature ostrich is capable of delivering a kick of up to 500 psi. A bicycle handlebar attached to a rake handle works well to fend off ostriches.

He wasn't sure exactly when the good-humoured jibes in the pub seemed to take on an edge. Lately he had noticed caps converging conspiratorially on seeing him enter, heard half whispers, caught the exchange of meaningful glances.

About to go out one Saturday evening, he turned back and sat down at the kitchen table, without removing his coat. Visualising rows of grinning faces hovering in the dark recesses of the bar.

'Well, Ignatius. Any news? Have those birds still not kittled yet?'

'Are you sure they're not all fellas? Ay Ignatius? Maybe there was a mix up and they sold you four of the same!'

'Ah be fair ... they're just a bit sensitive. All they want's a bit of candlelight and nice music to put them in the mood!'

There was a swell of laughter like a tidal wave. It swept over him where he sat, spotlit on his lone stool at the bar, trying to smile, sweat glinting on his upper lip.

So he sat instead at his kitchen table, unscrewed the bottle of whiskey from the night before and poured himself a large glass, not bothering to add water. He sat there till it grew dark. Till he had stopped being afraid for a while.

Some nights the Ostrich had a dream. He was in a huge landscape under a hallucinatory sun. The burnt earth sweet as toast under his feet. The only sounds the dry skittering of insects across the dust, the whispering rattle of seed pods falling from distant trees, the low creak of baked rocks expanding. The vermilion sun burned out at last and slid behind the purple mountains till darkness enveloped him. And a billion stars gleamed above him, rippling his feathers with their icy light.

He awoke and the narrow sky was bleached grey, all the colours had run dirty and the cold ground was sodden.

Most mornings lately Ignatius found himself stumbling to the paddocks, empty bottle in hand. He would stand for a while, looking at the four grey birds gaping dumbly in the open under a full downpour. He tried in vain to look into their eyes for clues. He had been able to read the cattle's honest brown eyes, to lay a hand on their warm flanks, listen to their breathing, calm and trusting in the morning air. He glanced over at the old hay barn that now stood redundant, its sides already caving in with neglect, and he felt a profound nostalgia. He recalled how the cattle listened to his sympathetic murmurs, lowering their heads to be caressed. But the bald, alien heads that bobbed in front of him told him nothing and the wide, staring eyes reflected nothing. Nothing but the void of wilderness, of rock. And in their indifference was a kind of enmity.

Once the bird is hooded, it should settle down and be much easier to handle. A sheet of plywood, with holes for the arms to pass through, protects the handler who is placing a hood over the Ostrich's head.

After lifting himself painfully out of bed, Ignatius lifted the kettle onto the stove with difficulty. His ribs hurt and he hadn't managed to eat properly for the last few days. He felt weak and disorientated. The deep scratches on his arm weren't healing. He stumbled against the range and groaned at the pain. The motion dislodged a small card from the cluttered shelf above. Details of the local vet. He held the card in his hand for ages before limping over to the phone and dialling the number.

Corrigan looked him up and down when he climbed out of his car.

'Have you injured yourself?' he inquired, noticing how Ignatius held his arm against his ribs as he limped to the paddocks beside him.

'Ah, nothin' too serious,' Ignatius muttered. 'Comes with the territory.'

The ostriches gathered close to the fence, surveying them with the forward nosiness of long-term inmates.

'So, they've been showing no kantling behaviour?' Corrigan asked. 'No mating displays at all?'

'Nothing. It's been months now ... the season's nearly over.'

Corrigan squinted into the paddock, shook his head. 'Aye, that's the way it goes, sometimes.'

'I've done all I can do. I'm ... I'm comin' to my wits end.' Ignatius hadn't meant to be so confessional but he hadn't spoken to another human being for some weeks.

Corrigan pursed his lips as he surveyed the emaciated, dishevelled figure beside him.

'I can see that. You look like you could do with a doctor yourself, Ignatius.'

Corrigan walked around the paddocks, asked a few more questions about the birds' general behaviour, about whether Ignatius had been attacked by any of them, looking askance at his injuries as he did so.

'I got lit on by the older one there ... my own fault. I went in without any protection to check the feeder ... thought they were all secure,' Ignatius mumbled, a bit shame faced.

'My God, you were lucky enough. Men have been killed

by a kick from these brutes.' The vet shook his head. 'D'ye know, they're strange animals, these birds. I've even heard of them forming an attachment to their owners, instead of to their mates.'

Ignatius stared at Corrigan, whose expression seemed to him suddenly sly and subtly mocking.

'I wonder now ... it would explain the lack of eggs.' Corrigan scratched his chin.

'How do you mean?' Ignatius felt a dropping sensation in the pit of his stomach.

'It can happen. The stupid things, well, they sort of fall in love with their owner.' Corrigan didn't look at Ignatius. 'So when he appears, they puff out their wings and run after him because they think he's their mate.'

The feeling was becoming a deep, shameful burning through Ignatius's sore ribs.

'And the owner cheers to himself because he thinks the birds are being territorial and chasing him off to get down to business when he leaves,' Corrigan continued cheerfully. 'But when he leaves, in fact they just stand around and pine for *him*. Recent case of that in Scotland.' Corrigan shook his head and laughed. 'I'll tell you, though, you wouldn't want to be the heart's desire of an ostrich in love!'

Hopelessly, Ignatius felt fate irrevocably asserting itself. Sensed the forming of a huge, inescapable joke, with him trapped like a beetle at its centre.

Corrigan winced at Ignatius's grim face, coughed awkwardly, grew serious again.

'Of course, we can rule out anything like that here. Usually only happens with birds hand-reared from birth, and sure these were already a couple of years old when you got them.' He kept talking but Ignatius only heard snatches of what he was saying. 'Could be a number of environmental reasons: weather, temperature ... can't see any physical reason myself ...'

He said something else about luck of the draw and here's hoping for next year. To keep an eye on them and keep him informed. And to go see a doctor.

Ignatius watched the expensive-looking four by four exit his gate and recede down the lane. And he knew in his heart that his reputation went with it. That his future was circumscribed by the absurdity of his failure. And his heart felt as brittle as an empty shell.

Ignatius got up late the following morning. It was raining again. He went to replace the kettle on the stove and knocked his cup off the kitchen table onto the floor. He stared at the clean blue and white shards on the dark lino and the blue made him think of the new blue rope he had bought. Strong nylon rope for securing the fence posts around the ostrich paddocks. He went into the back room and got a good length of the rope. Then he crossed the yard to the lonely barn, entered it and closed the door behind him.

The ostriches stalked restlessly around their paddocks, aware of the strange new silence that enveloped the farm. They stood in the rain and waited. And waited.

But no one came. And soon nothing punctuated the beginning of one day and the ending of another. Except the rising of the sun in the morning and the setting of the sun at night. The feed ran out. The drinkers were drained of water. And the sun rose and set again. One night the stars hung low in the sky and the Ostrich looked out at them. In their cool, winking light there was an ancient familiarity, the hint of something once known, but somehow lost. The Ostrich stared unblinking at the sky full of stars. Bright and beautiful, they reflected empty light, revealing nothing.

Eileen Brannigan is currently completing a first collection of short stories.

SPLENDENT SUN
AND TAWNY MOON

Dermot MacCormack

Dermot MacCormack was short-listed for a Hennessy First Fiction Award in 1996. Since then he has finished a collection of stories called *The Philadelphians* and is working on a novel set during the First World War. He has been published in *Irish Edition*, *Irish Echo* and *Scan Magazine*, and currently works in Philadephia, teaching graphic design at Temple University. (2004)

Once, there was a time when I could fly but that was long ago. Now I am too old and, besides, I don't have the need to fly anymore like I used to.

When I was young I stood over six feet tall and my wings when outstretched spanned over fourteen feet across. When I tucked them in close to my back the scapulars stood high over my head and shoulders, making me seem even taller. Anyone who saw them was struck with awe. Children, especially, would sometimes come up to me and gently touch my chestnut coloured feathers. Parents would sometimes stand back, shy yet anxious; a little afraid, I suppose. An audible gasp would come from them all when I stood up, spread my wings and effortlessly took off into the skies. I would look down at them, the children waving and squealing while the parents would peak their hands over their eyes, trying to follow my path through the glare of the splendent sun. It was a wonderful feeling although at the time, I suppose, I took it all a bit for granted.

I remember the first time I flew back home. My mother and father, God bless their souls, stood in the centre of a field of barley. I pushed my wings forward in front of me as I descended. It was the softest of landings and I stood there before them smiling. They were both so pleased and proud to see me. My mother stood with her hands covering her mouth; she was so excited. My father gave me his usual strong handshake and, tired as I was, I told them of my long trip across the Atlantic. My mother's eyes widened when I told her of the sights I had seen in Newfoundland, of the bitter cold in Greenland, and she laughed heartily when I told her of the children who gathered around me in the harbour of Reykjavik.

As I sat in the kitchen, or rather my kitchen now, I should say, I was very touched to see neighbours and friends come to visit, people I had not seen for a long, long time. My father asked me why I had waited so many years to come back, even for a visit. I told him I simply didn't know. One thing leads to another and all that.

Feeling warm in the glow of the kitchen, I promised there and then to visit home once a year.

'You mean, you're going to migrate?' said Mr. Colgan jokingly, and everyone laughed, including myself.

Huh, where are they all now?

At first, I decided that to go home for the winter months was the thing to do but the weather across that cold ocean was too much. No matter how many layers of clothing I put on or no matter how fast I flew, I could never get used to it. So, after the second year I decided to go home during the summer months. My parents were usually in better form, people were home for the holidays and the rain was soft and intermittent. Not to mention that the heat in Philadelphia was oppressive, to say the least.

I will always remember that one particular trip I took as I flew high over the Cliffs of Moher. The thick cumulus clouds suddenly parted and below me the vast patchwork of green fields stretched out before me like a newly woven quilt. I don't know why it struck me so. I had, of course, seen it many times before but there was something about the light that day, the colours of the fields, the blueness of the waves beneath me, that nearly took my breath away. There, in the sky, I felt like a child again.

Over the years, the neighbours gradually stopped coming to visit when I arrived; the novelty had worn off, I suppose. And then that terrible day as I descended in wide circles following the cool currents. There, alone in the field, stood my mother dressed in a floral dress.

Maybe it was best that he had died so suddenly but there was so much I still wanted to say.

Why did my mother not want me to move back? I have often wondered that. Perhaps all along it was he who really wanted me home. I don't know really. After all, I had no special skills except that I could fly but, as my mother used to say, flying wouldn't plough the fields.

Still, I tried. I lifted the heavy machinery for the labourers. I could lift the bales of hay onto the trailers. Come to think of it, I even tried to sow some seeds but it was too erratic. The windblown seed falling everywhere but where it was supposed to. That day my mother laughed and I stood beside her and pulled her close under my wing even though I could feel that she suddenly became uncomfortable. I know she loved me – she just had a hard time telling me.

And then the phonecall in the night. My heart thumped hard against my ribs. I thought I would never reach home. I hardly stopped in St Johns or Tasiilaq even though the autumn winds blew right through me.

The field was unkempt, long empty drills now, curving over the hill.

Only two of the old neighbours attended the funeral and I didn't recognise anyone else who stood there in the wet afternoon at her graveside. No one greeted me when I landed that last time, only a dog barked. He stopped when I folded in my wings and as I looked straight at him he cocked his head sideways.

I wonder what my friends really thought when I phoned to say that I wouldn't be coming back? I'm sure they half expected it. All that arranging to sell everything and then having to ship the furniture. What an ordeal that was.

Soon, over time, I fitted in, I suppose. Every once in a while I would fly the short distance to the village to pick up the groceries. Some of the new children from the housing estate would run up to me but I didn't have the strength like I used to. I tried to take some of the smaller ones on a short flight, more like a jump really, over to the roundabout but the parents were not too thrilled and, to be honest, my heart wasn't in it either.

I stopped flying altogether soon after that. I kept my wings tucked in close behind me. Eventually I had to tie them with a wide sash, which I bought in Cambells, in order to keep them secure. Then, I suppose, my muscles couldn't do it any longer. The operation was really quite painless when I think of it. They asked me in the hospital if I wanted to keep them and I'm glad that I did. Many's the hours I spent in front of the fire looking at them neatly arranged on a white sheet in that beautiful wooden box which old Mr Bellew made for me.

I did not feel saddened by them. Quite the contrary really. They held so many memories for me and much more good than bad. They were a connection to many things.

But as they say all good things must come to an end. I wonder what my mother and father would say now? They never thought, I suppose, that one autumn evening, I would be standing in our garden burning my God-given wings on a fiery pyre.

It is such a still evening today. The rust coloured smoke is going almost straight up. Straight up, through the dim light of the tawny moon.

Dermot MacCormack's story received The Hennessy Writer of the Year Award in 2005.

The *Pamela Anderson*

Pól MacReannacháin

Pól MacReannacháin was born in Derry.
After graduating from the University of
Manchester he worked for a few years
before leaving to travel in Italy. He now
lives in Strabane, where he grew up. 'The
Pamela Anderson' is his first story. (2004)

*A*rt gallery audio-guide:
Moving on, just to the right of
this, we come to perhaps what is one
of the most famous pre-war works of
portraiture. It is, of course, the un-
mistakable Pamela Anderson by an
unknown artist.

The portrait, an example of *fin de
siècle* twentieth century photography,
was discovered late in the twenty-third
century during the clearance of the
Los Angeles ruins, and was donated to
the gallery as a goodwill gesture by the
government of the East Pacific Free
State. It is certainly a remarkable piece
and has generated a great deal of com-
mentary and controversy.

We actually know very little about who the real Pamela Anderson was. The Great War that arose from the War on Terror proved to be a conflagration of such intensity that much American art and its derivations were destroyed in the various purges and re-education programs. One can only assume that she was a figure of some nobility, possibly a person who wielded a degree of power. It can be surmised that she commanded a great deal of respect and was revered by a great many people. The lack of annotation – only her name is present along the bottom of the portrait – adds further credence to the supposition that she was a figure familiar to many and needed no introduction.

In this piece, we see the eponymous Pamela Anderson, a pre-miscegenate Caucasian female, reclining on a large white bed. To our eyes a pre-miscegenate individual may seem peculiar, but we must remember that prior to the establishment of the Grand Council, people tended to reproduce with members of the same race, and miscegenation began out of expediency, to counteract the falling population numbers resulting from the Great War.

Let us consider this famous portrait, a reproduction of which you have probably seen before. Pamela Anderson is undoubtedly the sole focus of the portraitist. There are no background or foreground elements and she is not surrounded by any objects, unless one takes into consideration the white bed. Therefore, one must deduce by inference the meaning of this piece.

Firstly, let us consider the colour scheme. What is immediately striking is the photographer's bold use of light, illuminating the subject so that not only does she dominate the frame, she seems to exude a radiance of her own. In the portrait, Pamela Anderson is placed on a white background, the silk sheets of a bed, and her body seems to glow with light. The colour white has traditionally been seen as the colour of purity. But in the Christian culture from which this portrait has been dated, white was also the symbolic colour of virginity. So we can surmise that Pamela Anderson occupied the role of a religious icon, perhaps of chastity. This makes the discovery of this piece all the more remarkable when one considers the anti-Christian purges of the Mahdi's troops as they conquered what is now the West Atlantic Alliance and the East Pacific Free State, during their conflict with what was then the short-lived state of the USA.

The powerful religious overtones of the *Pamela Anderson* are exacerbated by the full frontal nudity of the subject. It is difficult for us, perhaps, to imagine in our present age, but prior to the defeat of the Mahdi and the establishment of the Grand Council, the female form was a subject of contention and prejudice. Indeed, much has been said concerning how the purges of the Mahdi's troops were partially fuelled by a misogynistic desire that the female form should remain covered, despite the wishes of the individual woman. As the central conflict of the Great War was the mutually damaging struggle between Christianity and Islam, the nudity of *Pamela Anderson* may be taken to be representative, not only as a religious symbol, but also as a political statement of anti-Mahdi philosophy. Certainly, the location of the portrait – the craters of California, a site of pronounced aggression by the Mahdi's forces – points to this work being part of a culture in opposition to the Mahdi.

As such, it has been proposed that Pamela Anderson was a prominent figure in the resistance against the Mahdi's forces and may have been a guerrilla leader. Her iconic representation in this portrait is comparable with that of the Argentinean revolutionary Che Guevara, a figure from an earlier and better-recorded conflict in the now obliterated Caribbean island of Cuba. Equally, she may have been fulfilling a purely symbolic role and acted as a figurehead for the rebels besieged by the Mahdi's troops. In this way, she can be compared to that other female voice of resistance: *La Passionaria*, who during the Spanish Civil War of the early twentieth century made the cry of '*No Pasarán!*' a rallying call for anti-fascist forces.

However, there is a further layer to the enigma of this portrait. The entire world culture from which the Great War erupted had a profound bias against women. In the Islamist culture that created the Mahdi, women were regarded as the property of men and had to wear robes that not only hid their bodies, but even the shapes of their bodies. The Christian culture was marginally more lenient, but women were still not afforded parity of esteem with their male counterparts. So the *Pamela Anderson* may also be a statement, not only against the attitudes of the Mahdi and his followers, but of the culture of Los Angeles; itself a Christian enclave.

In this way the portrait of Pamela Anderson can be read not only as a deeply religious and political icon, but as a condemnatory reply to the patriarchal culture that considered the female body shameful; something that had to be hidden.

Thus, we are presented with a most enigmatic figure, luminous on her white bed with her glowing skin and gleaming hair, from one of the darkest periods of our history. We may be able to catalogue with some degree of accuracy the pre-war history of world conflict up until the War on Terror, when media obfuscation began to create a chaos of confusion. But of the years between the War on Terror and the end of the Great War, we must confess our ignorance. It is only via examples of high art such as the portrait you see before you that we can glimpse a lost world of passionate beliefs and idealism.

Finally, one cannot speak of the *Pamela Anderson* without dwelling on that famous and endlessly mysterious smile. For generations it has given scholars, historians, art critics and pundits pause for thought. Just what is Pamela Anderson smiling at? It is, of course, a question that is impossible to answer; indeed, it is a question *without* an answer. Her famous smile, like that of the Sphinx, provides us with a tantalising riddle. One is free to make one's own deductions, but in this critic's opinion the famous smile of *Pamela Anderson* is intimately bound up with the portrait as a religious, political and social call to arms.

Because it is a smile directed at nothing in particular, it is a smile directed at everything in general. And I think that this adds an interesting dimension to the piece. It is a smile directed at the whole of humanity. Friend or foe, the viewer is greeted with a smile from this powerful, politicised religious icon. As such it represents one of the greatest examples of Christian art from the ultimate epoch of this once great religion, a religion that taught its followers to love their neighbours, their enemies and themselves.

Perhaps in her famous smile, Pamela Anderson was reminding Christians of their true vocation, demonstrating the core Christian moral of pacifism and love for humanity. In this way, *Pamela Anderson* represents a powerful Christian message, akin to that of the historical figure of St Francis of Assisi, and may have been seen as an *Alter Christus* by her admirers. If so, and I think it is, it may have been her smile that, on the eve of war, prevented the *Pamela Anderson* from going on public display.

At a period of great religious and political turmoil, the deeply pacifist and philosophical nature of this portrait probably would have led to its suppression, and it is unlikely that this portrait was viewed widely upon its unveiling. It may very well have been its banishment into storage that spared it the brutal scourings of the Mahdi's purge. And I'm sure that's something we can all smile about.

Press the Pause button on your headset and take a few

moments to contemplate the *Pamela Anderson*. Then, when you're ready, press Play and move on to the right where we will see an example of early post-war art.

Pól MacReannacháin is currently working on a collection of short stories.

HENNESSY LITERARY AWARDS

LIST OF WINNERS

YEAR	WINNERS
1971	Patrick Buckley, Kate Cruise O'Brien, Desmond Hogan, Vincent Lawrence, John Boland, Dermot Morgan, Liam Murphy
1972	Fred Johnston, Ita Daly, Maeve O'Brien Kelly, Patrick Cunningham
1973	John Flannagan, Niall MacSweeney, George O'Brien, Brian Power
1974	Donall MacAmhlaigh, Dermot Healy, John MacArdle, Ronan Sheehan
1975	Edward Brazil, Ray Lynott, Lucile Redmond, John A. Ryan
1976	Robin Glendinning, Ray Lynott, Ita Daly, Dermot Healy, Thomas O'Keefe, Sean O'Donovan
1977	Denis Byrne, Michael Feeney Callan, John O'Leary, Joseph Nesson
1978	Patrick Doyle, M.J. Lally, Jim Lusby, Andrew Tyrrell
1979	Mary O'Shea, Alan Stewart, Patrick McCabe, Harry McHugh
1980	David Irving, Paul Hyde, Deirdre Madden, Michael Harding
1981	Briege Duffaud, Catherine Coakley, Gabrielle Warnock, Elizabeth O'Driscoll
1982	Eoghan Power, Anne Devlin, Rose Doyle, Anne Gilmore
1983	Maurice Power, Jim McCarthy, Brigid Flaherty, John MacKenna

1984	Frances Dalton, Ronan O'Callaghan, Vincent Mahon, Bill Hearne
1985	Shane Connaughton, John Grenham, David Liddy, Brian Lynch
1986	Peter McNiff, Keith Collins, Andrew E. Duffy, Colm Ó Clubháin
1987	Mary Byrne, Geraldine Meaney, Áine Miller, Mairide Woods
1988	Dermot Bolger, Maire Holmes, Ivy Bannister, James Leo Conway
1989	Joseph O'Connor, Julian Girdham, Sam Burnside
1990	Colum McCann, Maeve Kennedy, Mary O'Malley
1991	Cathy O'Riordan, Colm Keena, Ted McNulty
1992	Mike Philpott, Mairide Woods, Sheila O'Hagan
1993	John Galvin, Mary Arrigan, Vona Groarke
1994	Marina Carr, Martin Healy, Noelle Vial
1995	Eleanor Flegg, Kerry Hardie/Iggy McGovern, Michael Taft
1996	Gerry Beirne, Martina Devlin, Iggy McGovern
1997	Micheal Ó Conghaile, Rosita Boland, Aida Rooney-Cespedes
1998	Paul Perry, Philip Ó Ceallaigh, John O'Donnell
1999	Liz McSkene, Alys Meriol, Fiona O'Connor
2000	Geraldine Mills, Kieran Byrne, Pat Maddock, Desmond Traynor
2001	Mary O'Donoghue, Ronan Blaney, Philip Ó Ceallaigh
2002	Alan Monaghan, Patricia Beirne, Lindsay Hosges
2003	Seamus Keenan, Sinead McMahon, Jennifer Harrington-Sexton
2004	Terry Donnelly, Laurence O'Dwyer, Dermot MacCormack

HENNESSY LITERARY AWARDS

LIST OF JUDGES

YEAR	JUDGES
1971	Elizabeth Bowen, William Trevor
1972	Brian Friel, James Plunkett
1973	Sean O'Faolain, Kingsley Amis
1974	Edna O'Brien, V.S. Pritchett
1975	Brian Moore, William Saroyan
1976	Alan Stillitoe, Aidan Higgins
1977	Melvyn Bragg, John McGahern
1978	John Braine, Mary Lavin
1979	Julia O'Faolain, John Wain
1980	Bryan MacMahon, Penelope Mortimer
1981	Heinrich Böll, Terence de Vere White
1982	Jennifer Johnston, D.M. Thomas
1983	Victoria Gleninning, Benedict Kiely
1984	Molly Keane, John Mortimer
1985	Bernard MacLaverty, Robert Nye
1986	Frank Delaney, Judy Cooke
1987	Douglas Dunn, John Montague
1988	David Marcus, Ian McEwan
1989	Piers Paul Read, Brendan Kennelly
1990	Clare Boylan, Desmond Hogan
1991	Fay Weldon, Neil Jordan
1992	Wendy Cope, Hugh Leonard
1993	Penelope Lively, Ita Duffy
1994	Beryl Bainbridge, Dermot Bolger
1995	Edna O'Brien, Joseph O'Connor
1996	Justin Cartwright, Deirdre Madden

1997	Roddy Doyle, Patrick Gale
1998	Micheal Ó Siadhail, Jennifer Johnston
1999	Marina Carr, Colm Tóibín
2000	Colm McCann, Andrew O'Hagan
2001	Anne Enright, Ole Larsom
2002	Patrick McGrath, Bernard Farrell
2003	Patrick McCabe, Bernice Rubens
2004	Frank McGuinness, Ronan Bennett